The Triangle
Book 4 in The
Castleton Series

Written by Mike Dunbar

Illustrated by Sara Santienello

ISBN-13: 978-1494404819

ISBN-10: 1494404818

DEDICATION

To my wife, the real Allie Tymoshenko.

CONTENTS

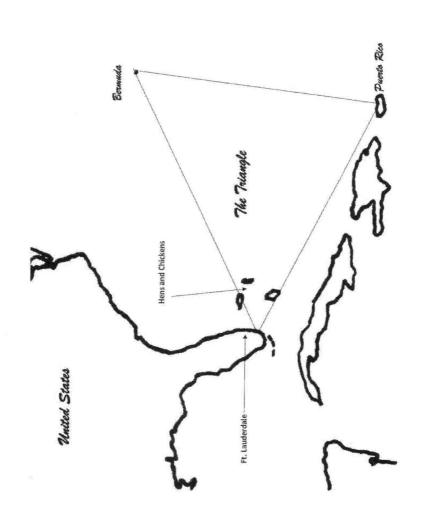

The Triangle

CHAPTER ONE
FLIGHT 19

Lieutenant Chuck Newcomb entered the door of the officers club at Naval Air Station Fort Lauderdale. The 25 year old Navy pilot had just eaten lunch and planned to finish it off with some coffee. He walked to a table and poured himself a cup. Next, the tall, thin pilot picked up a red crayon and drew a dark red line through the date on the calendar – December 5, 1945. He sat down in an upholstered arm chair and took a long sip of his coffee. "One less day before you become a free man," said Lieutenant Charlie Taylor, sitting in the next chair. Like Chuck, Lt. Taylor was wearing tan slacks and a tan, short-sleeved shirt. This was the uniform Navy officers wore when they were on duty.

"Yup," replied Lt. Newcomb. "Less than six months now. I can't wait for May 1 when my enlistment is up and I say goodbye to the Navy. I should be able to get back home to Baltimore before my wife has the baby. This is our first and I want to be there with her."

"You'll miss flying," said Lt. Taylor, teasing his friend. "You'll miss Navy food and Navy coffee."

"Not much," Lt. Newcomb answered. "My wife's a great cook and she makes much better coffee. As for flying, I'm going to apply for a job with TransAmerican Airlines. Now that the war is over they're buying old Army and Navy DC 3s. They're turning those military gooney birds into passenger planes. The company figures they can sell plane tickets as cheap as the trains, and get people where they're going a lot faster. I think they're right. Flying will be the way people travel in the future. I want to get in on the ground floor."

"There are gonna be a lot of military pilots looking for jobs," Lt. Taylor replied. "Jobs flying passenger planes are gonna be hard to get."

"I'm figuring I have a leg up," Lt. Newcomb said. "I teach flying. After all those missions I flew during the war the Navy made me a trainer. You know, you're a trainer too. You should think about flying passenger planes, Taylor. TransAm pilots make   good money."

"We teach pilots to fly Avenger bombers," Lt. Taylor argued. "We dive straight down until we almost crash into a ship. We drop a bomb and then fly straight up again. We'd have more luck getting a job running a roller coaster. TransAmerican doesn't want the kind of flying we do."

"Suit yourself," Lt. Newcomb answered. "I'm applying for the job. Don't come knockin' on my door lookin' for a loan when I'm a rich, successful airline pilot."

The two flyers laughed.

"Can I get you to do me a favor, Chuck?" Lt. Taylor asked after a short pause.

"Sure," Lt. Newcomb answered. "What is it?"

"I'm supposed to take up Flight 19 and test them on Navigation Problem Number One," Lt. Taylor said. "You know, I gotta watch a bunch of trainees take a combination of bombing and navigation tests. I had a late night and I'm dead tired. Would you take my place? It's a piece of cake. These guys have a lot of experience and a trainee will lead the flight. You just have to watch 'em and make sure they don't get lost."

"Can't help you out, Buddy," Lt. Newcomb said, slowly shaking his head. "You're scheduled for Flight 19 at 1:45. I take up Flight 23 at 4:00 for the same test. If I fly your mission, I won't be back in time for mine."

"Guess I'd better have another cup of coffee," Lt. Taylor said with resignation. "That's the only way I'll stay awake. From now on I gotta get to bed earlier. Well, I better get to the ready room or I'll be late for the flight."

Lt. Newcomb relaxed in his chair as his friend stood up and poured himself a cup of coffee. Lt. Taylor put on his officer's cap and left the officers club, coffee in hand.

Lt. Newcomb still had a couple of hours of free time. He took out his wallet and opened it to a picture of his wife. He gazed lovingly at her. He kissed the picture and returned the wallet to his pocket. He put his head back on the chair and soon, he was asleep.

In his dreams he was back at his home in Baltimore. He was playing ball with his young son. The baby would not be born for six months and could just as well turn out to be a girl. However, in Chuck's dream it was the son he wanted so badly. He named the boy Charles, just like his father and grandfather. However, in his dream he called the boy Junior. He could tell from the way the boy threw the ball, Junior Newcomb was a natural athlete, a natural ball player. He would be a pitcher. There was no doubt he would play in the major leagues - for the Baltimore Orioles. He would lead his team to the World Series and win the final game with his brilliant pitching.

"Lieutenant! Lieutenant Newcomb," a distant voice called urgently. "Lieutenant, Sir. Wake up." Chuck Newcomb opened his eyes. He was surprised to see a sailor standing in front of his chair. The only enlisted men allowed in the club were those that worked there. They were cooks and waiters and they all wore white jackets. Standing in front of him was an enlisted man, dressed in a pale blue denim shirt and dark denim work pants. What was an ordinary sailor dressed in work clothes doing in the officer's club? Chuck wiped the sleep from his eyes.

"Lieutenant Newcomb, Sir," the sailor said. "Lieutenant, they want you at the tower. Right away, Sir."

"Why," Lieutenant Newcomb asked as the last images of his dream disappeared like smoke. "What's the matter?"

"It's Lieutenant Taylor, Sir," the sailor said. "It's Flight 19. They're in trouble. You gotta get to the tower right away, Sir. This is an emergency."

Lt. Newcomb grabbed his officer cap and ran out the door. He was tall, thin and had long legs, so was able to run much faster than the sailor. When he reached the tower he ran up the stairs taking two steps at a time. He burst open the tower door. "What's happened to Lt. Taylor?" he demanded.

"Listen, Sir," the radio operator said.

Lt. Taylor's voice came from the speaker. "I don't know where we are," he said. "Fort Lauderdale. Can you see us on radar? Where are we?"

Another officer named Lt. Bob Fox was also in the tower listening to the messages from Flight 19. "One of my students received a transmission, Chuck," Lt. Fox said to Lt. Newcomb. "I was taking up Flight 20. We were ready to take off to do Navigation Problem Number One. A voice on the radio asked my student what his compass reading was. We didn't know if the message was coming from a boat or a plane. We asked the caller to identify himself. He said his name was Powers and he was with Flight 19.

"A while later we heard another call. This one was Lt. Taylor. He said both of his compasses were out and he was trying to find Fort Lauderdale, Florida. He said he was over land but it was broken patches, like islands. He thought he was in the Keys, but he didn't know how far down. He asked how to get to Fort Lauderdale. I came up here to the tower to report what we had heard. The tower had gotten the same messages."

Now, things got really crazy. Taylor's voice came over the radio. "Fort Lauderdale. My instruments are spinning."

Chuck Newcomb took the radio microphone. "Taylor," he said. "This is Chuck. Forget your instruments. It's afternoon. The sun is in the west. Turn the planes so you are facing it. That will bring you back to land."

"I can't see the sun," Lt. Taylor answered. He sounded scared. "It's like we're in a cloud. I can't see anything. I can see the other planes as clear as day. So, I know we're not in a cloud. I just can't tell where the light's coming from. Everything else has disappeared. I don't know how to find up or down. Without instruments I'm afraid we're gonna crash into the sea. We don't know where the sea is."

Chuck Newcomb turned to the sailor who had awakened him in the officer's club. "Get down to the hanger," he said. "Have the crew get my plane ready. Find Ensign Dubois. Tell him he's flying with me as my radioman." He turned to Lt. Fox and said, "I'm going out to find Taylor and his flight. I need you to stay here in the tower and keep in radio contact with me. Let me know if you receive any more messages and tell me what they are.

"Taylor's a good pilot," Lt. Newcomb continued. "He and his flight are close to where they should be. It just sounds like his instruments have stopped working. If you stay here and keep in touch with me on the radio," Lt. Newcomb said as ran out the door, "you should be able to lead me right to him." On the way down he again took the stairs two at a time. He was running across the runway when Lt. Fox yelled down to him from the tower. "Why aren't the instruments working in the other planes?" Lt. Newcomb was too far away to hear.

Chuck ran into the ready room. There he put on his pilot's coveralls and pulled a tight fitting leather helmet over his head. The helmet had a radio speaker over one ear so he could hear radio messages. He strapped on his bright yellow, inflatable life preserver and grabbed his parachute. He threw the parachute over his shoulder so it looked like a back pack. He was half way out the door when he turned and went back to his locker. He took his pistol out of the metal cabinet and strapped it on his hip. He patted the gun like it gave him a sense of security. He didn't know why he would need a pistol, but going into a strange situation he just felt better with it.

Strapped into his plane's cockpit Lt. Newcomb used the plane's intercom to ask Ensign Dubois if he was ready for takeoff. The radioman's seat faced the plane's tail. In combat, he would have a machine gun to protect the plane from an enemy approaching from behind. However, this plane was a trainer and was unarmed. Chuck Newcomb gave a thumb up to the men on the runway to tell them he was ready to go. He began his taxi out to the end of the runway.

When he was in place for takeoff he gave his huge engine the gas. The engine roared and the propeller became a spinning blur. The big Avenger bomber started down the runway, rapidly gaining speed. Soon, the wheels left the ground and Chuck Newcomb pulled the plane's nose skyward to gain altitude. Then, he turned the plane eastward over the Atlantic Ocean and towards Hens and Chickens Shoals. Those were the tiny islands where the Navy practiced bombing. "He's still in that area," Lt. Newcomb said to Ensign Dubois, who was sitting behind him. "We'll be there in a half hour. We'll have Flight 19 back on the ground in time for supper."

"Chuck," a voice said over the radio. It was Lt. Fox. "We heard from Taylor again. He's still lost and says he can't see anything. I told him you were on the way. I told him to fly in circles. That way he stays in the area where he is."

"Good idea," Lt. Newcomb radioed back. "I don't need him flying off looking for land. I'll just end up in a wild goose chase. I'm going to fly zigzag through the area around Hens and Chickens. That way, if he's flying circles, we'll run into each other."

At that moment Lt. Newcomb heard a message on his radio from Taylor. "This is crazy," the frightened voice said. "Everything's crazy. What's going on? This can't be." Taylor sounded like he was about to break down from fear.

"Charlie," Chuck Newcomb called over his plane's radio to Taylor. "Charlie. Hold on. I'm almost there. Just keep flying in circles. I'll find you and lead you back." In five minutes Chuck Newcomb saw the small islands called Hens and Chickens. "Charlie, I'm here," he radioed. There was silence. "Charlie. Lt. Taylor. Flight 19. We've arrived. Talk to me. Someone talk to me." The radio remained silent.

"Ft. Lauderdale," Chuck Newcomb radioed. "Bob. Have you heard from Taylor?"

"No," Bob Fox's voice answered. "He hasn't radioed for 10 minutes. He sounded scared. We heard him say everything was crazy. He sounded like he was going crazy."

"If he didn't report he was going down I'm gonna guess he's still up here," Chuck replied. "Maybe his radio broke down too."

"Why aren't the other planes radioing, Chuck?" Bob Fox asked. "All their compasses and radios can't be broke. Why didn't the other planes lead Taylor back?"

"I don't know," Chuck replied. That was the first time he had thought about that question. Bob was right. All their instruments couldn't break down at the same time. That was crazy. Lt. Newcomb began to fly a pattern of zigzags over the small islands. He went west for a while, flying away from land. He then turned around to fly back east toward land. Each time, he moved a little more north. This way, he would eventually cover the entire area, and he would find Taylor. When he did, he would signal Flight 19 to follow him back to Naval Air Station Ft. Lauderdale and to safety.

Lt. Newcomb squinted as he scanned the sky in front of his plane. He turned his head and scanned the sky side-to-side. Meanwhile, Ensign Dubois scanned the sky behind the plane, as well as looking side-to-side. Between the pilot and the radio man, they could see the entire sky around the Avenger.

Other than Lt. Taylor, they didn't know the other flyers in those missing planes. Those were younger men learning to be bomber crews. However, Newcomb and Dubois had just finished fighting World War II and they had known hundreds of other flyers. Flyers were all like brothers. They took care of each other. Somewhere out there were five missing planes and 10 of their brothers. They knew that if they were the ones who were lost, each of those missing flyers would volunteer for the rescue mission.

Back at Naval Air Station Fort Lauderdale the radar man was watching Lt. Newcomb's plane on his radar screen. It appeared as a green blip. Suddenly, three more blips appeared right behind Lt. Newcomb. "Lt. Fox," the radar man said. "I think Lt. Newcomb has found some of Flight 19. Look here." He showed Lt. Fox the three new blips.

"Chuck," Lt. Fox said into the radio microphone. "Chuck. You're in luck. They found you. You have three planes on your tail. Can you identify them? Is Taylor one of them?"

"You see any planes behind us, Dubois?" Lt. Newcomb asked his radioman.

"Nothing there, Sir," Dubois answered.

"No planes behind us, Bob," Lt. Newcomb radioed back to Ft. Lauderdale.

Bob Fox and the radar man continued to stare at the blips. "They're right behind you, Chuck," he said. "If they were enemy planes they could shoot you out of the sky, they're so close."

"Nothing there," answered Lt. Newcomb's voice. "Dubois has a clear view behind the plane. There's nothing there. Maybe they're just ghost images."

"Sir," the radar man said to Lt. Fox. "I ran radar through the whole war. I know radar inside and out. Those are not ghost images, Sir. Those are craft. I don't know how Ensign Dubois can miss them. They're right in his face. If they got any closer they'd bump the plane."

"Taylor," Lt. Fox said into the radio microphone. "Do you see Lt. Newcomb's plane ahead of you?" There was no answer. "Any plane in Flight 19," he said. "Report. Do you see an Avenger just ahead of you?" Silence.

"Unidentified aircraft,'" Lt. Fox said into the radio. "You are in restricted air space. Identify yourself." There was no answer.

Chuck was scanning the sky straight ahead of the plane when he noticed his compass needle swing. It went to the right and then to the left. Then, it returned to its original position. Chuck ignored it. He was busy searching the sky. Five minutes later Ensign Dubois said, "Darned thing." He banged on his radio.

"What's up," Chuck asked.

"My radio just changed frequency. I'm not in touch with Ft. Lauderdale anymore. I'll adjust it. Ft. Lauderdale, do you read me?"

"Copy," said a voice, but it was very faint and nearly covered by static.

At that point Chuck Newcomb saw his compass needle swing again. This time it did not stop. In fact, it began to spin. He looked at the altimeter, a device that told the pilot how high he was. The altimeter is a very important instrument. In rain or fog a plane could fly into the ground without the pilot knowing he was too low. Like the compass, the Avenger's altimeter began to swing. "What's going on?" Lt. Newcomb asked out loud.

"Chuck," Ensign Dubois said. "Look at the sky. It's weird."

Ensign Dubois was right. Everything was gone. There were no clouds. There was no sun. He couldn't see the ocean, and he couldn't see the sky. Everything was gray. There was light, so Lt. Newcomb could see. There just wasn't anything to see. He held up his hand. It did not make a shadow. The light was not coming from anywhere, but it was everywhere. "I don't know what's happened, Dubois. I'm going to turn around and see if we can fly back out of this."

Chuck quickly realized that without instruments or anything to see, he wouldn't know when he had turned his plane around. He could go in a complete circle. He guessed and then, looked at his watch so he would know how long he flew in the new direction. His watch said 12:00. He knew it was about 4:00. "What time is it, Dubois," he asked his radioman.

"My watch is on the fritz," Dubois answered. "It says its 12:00. The second hand is on the 12 too. It's not moving."

"Tell Ft. Lauderdale we're having trouble," Lt. Newcomb told his radioman.

"Naval Air Station Ft. Lauderdale," Dubois said into his microphone. "This is TB Avenger 307. Ensign Dubois speaking. Ft. Lauderdale, we're having trouble. Our instruments are not working. Do you read me?"

"TB Avenger 307. I read you," said the voice. "What's your position?"

"We don't know," Dubois answered. "We were over the Hens and Chickens, but now we can't see anything."

"You must be over a cloud," the voice said. "Where's the sun?"

"There is no sun," Dubois answered. He realized he had just repeated almost word for word what Taylor had said, and realized he had the same fear in his own voice. "There is no nothing."

The voice replied, "Look for anyth…." It stopped in the middle of the word. The tower at Fort Lauderdale was gone. Within seconds the Avenger's engine began to sputter. It was shutting down. Chuck Newcomb tried to start it again. Nothing happened. Nothing in the plane worked. It was like all the electricity was gone.

"We're gonna have to bailout, Dubois," Newcomb yelled to his radioman. "I'll try to keep us gliding. Open the canopy." Dubois undid his safety harness and turned so he could reach forward. He unlocked the canopy, the curved windshield that covers the cockpit, and slid it back out of the way. Now, he and the pilot could climb up and jump away from the plane so they were not hurt, or get their parachutes tangled in the tail.

Standing with his head above the canopy Dubois said to the pilot, "There's no wind." The plane was moving so fast through the air that wind should be blowing on him like a hurricane. It was not. The air was calm.

"Don't be crazy," Chuck Newcomb answered. "If we weren't moving through the air, we would fall out of the sky. There has to be wind." He held his hand above the canopy, but he too could feel no wind. "What? How are we staying in the air?"

"Maybe we're not," Dubois answered. He climbed out of the cockpit and stepped carefully onto the wing. Still no wind, no vibration. It was like the plane was parked on the runway at Ft. Lauderdale. Dubois got on his stomach and looked under the wing. He could see nothing. He held on to the edge of the wing and slowly lowered himself down. When his feet reached the bottom of the plane he felt something hard, and tested his footing. He could stand. He took a step very carefully because he could not see any surface under his feet. He could only feel it, and didn't know where it might end. He was afraid he could step off an edge and fall. He took several more steps, still being very careful, but there were no problems.

"It's okay, Lieutenant," Ensign Dubois said to the pilot. Chuck Newcomb climbed out of the cockpit, slid down off the wing, and walked until he stood beside the radioman. Together, they walked a short distance in front of the plane. When they turned to look back at the bomber, it was gone. They looked around for it. When Ensign Dubois again spotted the plane it appeared to be below them. The plane was on its side. Well, it was not lying on its side, that's just how they saw it. They were not looking down on the cockpit like they would if they were above their craft. It was like they were standing beside the plane looking at it, but it was under them. Ensign Dubois took ahold of the strap on Lt. Newcomb's parachute. It was like he was afraid of losing his pilot.

"Look!" Chuck Newcomb said with so much surprise he almost yelled to the radioman. In front of them was a crew member from Flight 19. At least it looked like it could be a Navy flyer. The man was flat. He looked like a guy in a cartoon who gets run over by a steam roller and is pressed flat like a pancake. At first, Newcomb and Dubois thought the guy was dead, but there was no blood. Then, they saw the guy's mouth and eyes move. Next, he seemed to wave his arm. It looked like he was talking.

With Ensign Dubois still holding Lt. Newcomb's parachute, they stepped toward the man, but they were held back by an invisible cord, or a string. They heard a voice say, "Hey, that hurts. Who's pushing me?' The voice was Lt. Taylor's.

"Taylor," Chuck said pushing again on the invisible string. "Taylor. Where are you?"

"Right here," Taylor answered. "What the heck's pushing me? It hurts."

Another voice said, "This can't be. This can't be."

"That's right," Dubois said to Newcomb, holding even tighter to the strap. "This can't be. This is all impossible."

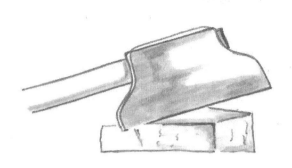

CHAPTER TWO
MARRAKECH

Aleksandra Tymoshenko, Lenore Smith, and Jen Canfield sat on a wall surrounding the Medina in the city of Marrakech. The Medina is the area enclosed by the city's fortifications. From their perch, the three time travelers were gazing down on the souk outside the city. A souk is a marketplace. This one was set up immediately against the city wall and was made up of rows of stalls covered with canopies.

The time was about 400 years before Columbus discovered America, and Marrakech was still a new city, less than 100 years old. However, the city had grown and because its Medina had already filled up with houses, people had begun to build outside the city wall. These newer suburbs were being built around the souk. In time, the marketplace would be surrounded by new buildings.

The three time travelers on the wall were the crew of the time craft Auckland. They were wearing time traveler uniforms that made them invisible to the crowd of people in the souk. From up on the wall they could watch, but not be seen.

The souk was a very busy place and merchants sold all sorts of things from their stalls. There was food. Some of it was raw, and was taken home to be cooked. Some it was cooked in the merchant's stall and was ready to eat. People bought this early North African version of fast food and snacked on it as they walked around the souk. Some merchants sold pots made of clay, while others stocked pots made of metal. The girls could see the hammer marks on the metal pots, showing that they had been created by hand.

Some merchants sold animals. There were chickens, ducks, and pigeons. There were sheep and calves. Some merchants sold clothing. Others had jewelry. There was a lot of gold in the jewelry stalls, especially rings. It seemed the people in Marrakech liked gold rings. In fact, the girls could see that everyone wore at least one ring. Some people had lots and lots of rings, many on every finger.

The souk was a loud place. All the animals complained about being in cages or tied up. People talked to each other in loud voices. It was so noisy there was only one way to be heard - yell. Merchants yelled at people walking past their stalls, trying to get their attention. Customers yelled to merchants even though they were close enough to touch each other.

The girls watched one merchant spread a rug on the ground in front of his stall for a customer to see. Meanwhile, another man led his donkey and cart across the rug. The rug merchant yelled loudly at the man with the cart. The cart man yelled back. The girls didn't understand, but they could tell the merchant was angry. The argument almost turned into a fight. Other men got involved and separated the donkey driver and the rug merchant. Everything settled down quickly and everyone went back to their business.

There was a lot of buying and selling. The girls couldn't understand what was being said, but they did notice nothing had a price tag. As they continued to watch they realized everyone was arguing over the price they wanted for their goods, or what they would pay. This type of bargaining is called haggling. It is very dramatic. The buyer asks the seller the price. The seller answers. Then, the buyer yells that the price is far too high. He claims he is just a poor man and cannot afford to pay that much. He waves his hands a lot to show how poor he is.

The seller yells that he paid more for the item than he is selling it for. He can't sell for any less. He is already losing money on the sale. The buyer comes up a bit on his offer and the seller comes down a bit on the price. Then, they both start yelling all over again about how poor they are. They do this several times until they make a deal. Finally, they bow to each other and kiss each other on the cheek. The girls watched a seller count his money and the buyer leave with his purchase. Both looked happy, like they had both come out on top. In fact, they both looked like they had enjoyed the haggling. All the haggling going on throughout the souk added a more than a fair share to the unending noise.

There was a lot of entertainment in the souk and that too added to the hubbub. Jugglers juggled all sorts of objects. There were acrobats and magicians. Small crowds gathered in front of each entertainer. A young boy or girl walked among the crowd holding a bowl. People in the crowd put small coins in the bowl to pay for the show they were watching.

The time crew was visiting Marrakech today for a reason. It was a spring festival. The shepherds and wandering desert tribes had come to the city for the celebration. It was easy to pick out the tribal people from the folk who lived in the city. Two generations ago an army of Arabs from Egypt had invaded and defeated the people of Marrakech.

The people who had built Marrakech and were defeated called themselves Berbers. It was easy to tell them from the victors. The Arabs that now lived in Marrakech wore white robes called djellabas, while the Berbers wore colorful robes, many of them deep blue. A lot of the Berbers had tattoos on their faces.

The war was long over and the two people now got along with each other. Some Berbers had begun to marry Arabs and the two people were in the process of becoming one. That's why the time team was here. They were a type of team called Researchers. Aleksandra was the team's science observer. That meant she traveled into the past and collected information for scholars doing research at the University of New Hampshire. Her specialty was music history. So, she usually helped scholars who studied music.

Berbers and Arabs played different kinds of music. As they became one people, their music was beginning to blend together. Aleksandra's job was to record music from this time in Marrakech so scholars could study the new music that was developing. The time crew had spotted a group of musicians gathering and knew they would soon start playing. For that reason, the three girls had chosen this spot above the crowd to make their recording. While they waited, they enjoyed the activities going on in the souk below.

Because they were on the wall above the crowd they noticed something strange before most of the people in the souk became aware of it. Two men were pushing their way through the crowd yelling loudly. The men were not dressed like anyone else. They wore single-piece suits of tan clothing that covered them from the ankles to the neck. They both had on bright yellow vests. They both wore a tight head cover with straps that hung over their cheeks. They had some object pushed up on their heads that reflected sunlight. The girls quickly realized the sun was reflecting off goggles.

The girls watched the men as they pushed their way closer to the wall. They were shouting, but not in Berber or Arabic. They were shouting, "Help. Help us. Where are we? Help." The time team was surprised to hear modern English, as the language didn't exist this early in history. Why was it being spoken here in northern Africa?

It was clear to the girls that the men were desperate and were in a state of terror, but the people in Marrakech didn't know that. They feared these excited men and guessed they were dangerous. Perhaps they were robbers, or they were assassins trying to kill someone important. The crowd closed in around the men to stop them. This frightened the men even more. One of them reached to his waist and pulled at something. The girls realized he had a pistol. He began waving it at the people yelling, "Get back! Get back! I'll shoot. I swear I'll shoot. Get away!"

Sure enough, he pointed the gun over the crowd's heads and pulled the trigger. The bullet hit a brass bell hanging from the Medina wall. The bell clanged and fell to pieces, hitting people nearby. That worked. The people were startled. They all ducked down and backed away from the men. However, it only worked for a minute. The crowd found its courage and closed in again on the strangers. The one with the pistol aimed it at the men in front of him. "Oh no," said Jen Canfield. "If he shoots people he'll change their sequences."

The guy with the gun didn't get the chance. Someone behind him hit him on the head with a clay pot. The pot broke and the man fell unconscious. The people grabbed the other man, who screamed and cried as he tried to kick his way free.

Soldiers armed with swords and spears pushed their way through the crowd. They were followed by older men with gray beards. The girls assumed these were city leaders. The soldiers seized the men and dragged them to a wooden post. They tied them to the stake while the crowd yelled at the leaders. They were all trying to tell the old men what had happened. One of the elders held his hand in the air and the crowd fell silent. He looked at a man he knew and invited him to describe what had just transpired.

When the man was done telling his story the older man pointed to the gun on the ground and told a soldier to bring it. He turned and walked back into the Medina with the other leaders following. "Allie, Lenore, follow them," Jen said. "We need to get that gun back. We can't leave it in this time period. I'll stay and watch over these two men. We have to rescue them and get them out of here. If not, all sorts of sequences are going to be changed. This is a Fixer team's job, but we're the only ones here, so it's up to us."

Lenore and Allie ran along the top of the wall until they reached the gate that led into the Medina. As they did, the man carrying the gun examined the object and accidentally pulled the trigger. Another shot went into the air causing the poor frightened man to toss the devilish thing to the ground.

Minutes passed before he got the courage to retrieve it. This time he carried it very carefully in his open palms as he followed the leaders. Still cloaked, Allie and Lenore followed closely behind the man.

The group entered a house that was bigger than all the surrounding homes. Its size indicated that someone very important lived there. The cloaked time travelers watched through an open window as the men sat on cushions around a low table. They could tell that the house belonged to the older man who had listened to the story about the two strangers. He opened a cabinet and told the soldier to put the gun in it. He then closed the door and locked it with a key. The man returned to the head of the table and began to confer with the others.

Back in the souk, Jen continued to watch the two strangers. Two guards stood by them. Some people continued to stare at the men, but most had gone back to their work, or were enjoying the entertainment. One of the two men tied to the post continued to scream and cry, while the man who had been hit with the pot slowly woke up. He tried to rub his aching head, but with his hands tied to the post he couldn't reach. Jen could hear him speak. "Dubois, Dubois. Calm down. Get a hold of yourself. You're a United States Naval officer. Act like one." Dubois calmed down a bit, but he was still scared and confused.

Night began to fall. As it grew dark, the people of Marrakech left the souk and returned to their homes in the Media. The two guards left the men unattended and went into a nearby small building. They came back out carrying a large block of wood and a very big axe. Jen thought to herself, "I know what they're planning for tomorrow morning. We have to get these guys out of here tonight."

The two men tied to the post also understood what the block and axe meant. The one named Dubois began to cry again. "This can't be happening. This can't be happening," he cried, rocking back and forth against his bonds.

Back at the house, Allie and Lenore watched the men eat their supper. Servants brought them plates of flat bread and olives. They dipped the bread into a creamy yellow paste and ate it. They popped olives into their mouths and spit the pits into bowls. They continued to talk, and at last, seemed to reach an agreement. After supper the group of men left the house, while the one who owned it stretched and yawned. He left the room and closed the door.

Allie and Lenore waited until the lamps were out and the house was dark. Then, they slipped on their night vision goggles so they could see. They climbed through the window and tiptoed to the cabinet. "What do we do?" Allie asked Lenore. "We could take the cabinet, but it's pretty big to carry across town."

"Nick taught me a trick," Lenore answered. She took a small tool kit from her belt and pulled out a thin object. She used the tool to pick the lock. She opened the cabinet door, reached in, and handed the gun to Allie. "I picked the lock. You carry the gun. I don't want to touch it." Allie had to pass the gun to Lenore when she climbed out the window, but took it back when they were both outside the house.

The two girls returned to the square and climbed back up on the wall to join Jen. "We have the gun," Allie said. "What about the men?"

"They're being guarded," Jen answered. "I think they're going to lose their heads tomorrow morning. See the block and the axe? We have to do something about those guards. Ideas."

"Easy," Allie answered. "We put them to sleep,"

"How?" Jen asked. "We sing them lullabies?"

"When I was in the hospital after being Demetrius' slave, I couldn't sleep at night," Allie said. "The doctors gave me pills to help me. I took them for a couple of nights, but I wanted to get over my fears by myself. So, I stopped swallowing the pills. Every night they gave me another pill, but I put it in my drawer. I took the pills with me when I left the hospital. I always bring a supply of them with me on missions, just in case I have to knock someone out."

"You should be a Fixer," Jen said.

"I do love one," Allie answered. "He's taught me a lot about solving problems." The girls watched as a guard took a drink from a leather bag. He then passed the bag to the other guard who lifted it over his head and took a long swig. "A wine skin," Allie said. "Muslims aren't supposed to drink wine, but these guys don't follow the rules. I know how to take care of our two guards."

Allie climbed down from the wall. Invisible to everyone but her two friends wearing night vision goggles, she walked quietly across the souk. She took some pills from her pocket and dropped them into the wine skin's opening. Then, she went back to the wall to keep watch with Lenore and Jen. Sure enough, the guards passed the bag back and forth a few more times. It didn't take long for the pills to work. The two guards yawned several times and then slowly slipped down to their knees. They fell deeply asleep and tumbled over onto the ground.

The two men tied to the post watched in astonishment as the guards passed out. The one named Dubois was so surprised he stopped sobbing. The other man began to work at the ropes, trying to untie them. "Dubois," he said. "Pull yourself together. Work yourself free."

As he spoke he heard a voice say in English. "I'll untie you." Then, three small young girls appeared. Dubois started to yell again. "Quiet," Jen said in her command voice. "You'll wake up the city." Dubois was so surprised at the order that he shut up.

"Don't ask any questions," Jen told the two men. "We don't have time to answer. We have a craft. We'll get you out of here." Dubois' friend lifted his crying companion by the arm and helped him walk. They followed the three girls out of the souk.

"Can you tell me who you are?" the man asked.

"My name is Jen. This is Lenore and Allie," Jen answered. "We're from the Time Institute."

"The what?" the man asked.

"You're asking too many questions," Jen said firmly. The man understood and remained quiet.

The group walked out into the desert that surrounded the city. Eventually, Jen stopped the group. She reached into her pocket and took out a small device. "Seventy four," she said.

The two men were startled to see a craft-like object appear and a door silently open. Dubois began to cry again. "This can't be real," he said as tears ran down his cheeks. "This can't be happening."

Jen climbed into the craft. "Welcome to the Auckland," she said to the men, waving them in. "Come aboard." The two full-sized men had to bend over to fit in the small craft. They were too tall to sit on the benches, so they squatted on the craft's floor.

Allie and Lenore squeezed in around the two large men. "Good thing Nick put a supercharger on the Auckland," Lenore said. "Without it, we wouldn't be able to carry these guys."

"Where are we going, Jen?" Allie asked. "Where do we take them?"

"I know how Mike feels," Jen replied. "He always wants to ask Rabbi Cohen and Dr. Newcomb for advice."

Dubois's friend perked up and said, "Dr. Newcomb? That's my name too."

"There must be a lot of you Newcombs," Allie said. "We keep running into them. All we need is for you to be named Charles."

"I am," Chuck Newcomb said. "My first name is Charles. My friends call me Chuck. I'm Lt. Charles Newcomb, United States Navy."

The girls looked at each other. "Not again," Jen said putting her hand on her forehead like she had a headache. "Lt. Newcomb, what is the last date you remember?"

"Today is December 5, 1945," Chuck answered. "I know because I crossed the day off the calendar in the officers' club. I'm less than six months from getting out of the Navy."

"You're not even close to 1945," Jen said. "Lieutenant, you're in for a shock. Lots of things are not what they are supposed to be."

"You're telling me?" Chuck said. "Things are so weird here Ensign Dubois has had a nervous breakdown. Nothing's what it's supposed to be."

"I don't know what you've experienced," Jen said. "All I know is you are not supposed to be in Marrakech. And, you're not supposed to know about us. Both things are creating a great big headache for me and my crew.

"We could take them back to 1945," Jen suggested to Lenore and Allie.

"We shouldn't act too fast," Allie advised. "We don't know how they got here or what sequences are involved. We could create a bigger mess.

"Lt. Newcomb," Allie said turning to Chuck. "I'm sorry. I know it seems rude for us to talk about you like this, but I'm afraid we have to. We know lots of things you don't. We know lots of things you wouldn't understand. Please be patient with us."

Turning back to her crewmates Allie continued, "Ensign Dubois needs medical help and Lt. Newcomb doesn't look too good either." The girls could see Chuck's hands and lips trembling. "I suggest we take them to the UNH Medical Center. That's where I was treated. The doctors there can cure them."

"They'll see things they shouldn't know about," Lenore warned.

"They already know a lot of things they shouldn't know," Allie responded. "We're in a mess. We can't fix all of the mess, but we can fix their problems. We should get them help first. Then, we'll need to get help for us. We need advice on what to do. We need to know how to fix all that these men have learned about us."

The Auckland's crew met with Dr. Newcomb and Rabbi Cohen in Room 307 at the MacDonald Center and Jen described what they had seen in Marrakech. She explained why they had brought Lt. Newcomb and Ensign Dubois back to the Time Institute. It seemed the right thing to do. "Rabbi Cohen and I agree," Dr. Newcomb said. "You couldn't leave the men in Marrakech. They would have been killed. That could have changed all sorts of sequences. Imagine what would have happened if that gun had remained in that time.

"We also agree that you couldn't risk returning them to their own time. We don't know anything about what happened to them. They needed medical attention, and for now, the Medical Center is the best place for them."

"However, we still have some serious problems," Rabbi Cohen said. "We have two men from the past who have now seen the future. If they return to their time, they could cause all sorts of problems. We need to research what happened to them. We need to know how they got to Marrakech. We need to find out what their time, their families and friends, think happened to them. If history records them as lost, they can't just be suddenly found. It would cause Chaos. Once again we're reminded that time travel messes with your mind."

"We need to be very careful," Dr. Newcomb added. "We can't make any decisions until we know everything. All of us know a Fixer Team that is very good at solving these sorts of problems." The Auckland's crew all nodded in agreement. Yes, Patrick and his team were the right choice for this mission. "Would you ladies mind going and getting Mr. Weaver and his crew?" Dr. Newcomb asked.

CHAPTER THREE
GEOMETRY CLASS

Mike Castleton and Nick Pope walked into their Geometry class carrying heavy back packs full of books. They were now freshman at Atlantic Academy High School and both had just turned 15 years old. Counting pre-school they had attended the Atlantic Academy grammar school for ten years. This was their first year of high school, but it was their eleventh year together. They had been friends since they were four years old.

Nick and Mike had changed a lot since the sixth grade, when they had been cadets at The Time Institute. They were no longer boys. They were becoming young men. Nick had grown quite tall. He was now almost six feet. He was still skinny and his hair was still out of control, like a major case of helmet hair. Nick had tried all sorts of products to make it behave. Finally, he had given up and just let his shaggy mop do what it wanted. It gave Mrs. Martin, the assistant principal, lots of reasons to punish him for breaking the high school's strict dress code. Hair was supposed to be neatly combed.

Nick was still quiet and shy. He didn't joke, and a lot of times he didn't get it when other people were joking with him. He always looked worried. He wasn't. He just looked that way.

Mike was well-built. He was now shorter than Nick, but his shoulders had become wider. He was thin, but had more muscle than Nick. As a young boy, Mike's face had been sprinkled with freckles and his head had been round like a soccer ball. As he became a young man, his head had become longer. His freckles had grown lighter and spread out as his face grew.

Mike had developed a thick head of dark brown hair. He liked his naturally curly hair and kept it carefully combed. He let it grow just long enough that it would curl into little twists on his temples. About that time, Mrs. Martin would order him to get a haircut and give him a detention.

Mike's deep blue eyes were still his most striking feature. He had long, dark eye lashes and thick eyebrows. The girls in class loved his eyes and often told him that eyes like that were wasted on a boy.

Even when he was young Mike had a good sense of humor. As he grew older he became even funnier. He could always find something to joke about, even in a serious situation.

Mike and Nick liked the high school. In grammar school they sat at desks and the teacher stood at the front of the class. Atlantic Academy high school used a different learning method. Here, the students and teacher sat around a large, oval table. The teacher didn't teach. Instead, he or she led a discussion. No one raised their hands. Each person spoke when he or she had something to add, or had a question to ask. The students debated with each other, and sometimes they even debated with the teacher. Teachers liked this. They wanted the students to challenge every idea and work out their own understanding   of life.

Today, the teacher, Mr. Li, was reviewing for a Geometry test at the end of the week. "What is a point?" he asked the class. Mr. Li was born in China and came to the United States as an adult. So, he spoke with a heavy accent. At first, he was hard to understand, but it was now October and the students had gotten used to his unusual speech patterns.

Mr. Li was the head of the math department at Atlantic Academy. Everyone knew he was the best math teacher in the school. He even had been offered a job teaching at nearby Poindexter Academy. Poindexter was a bigger school than Atlantic Academy and all the kids were rich. They had the best of everything, but they did not have Mr. Li.

"A point is something that has no length, width, or height," a boy named JR answered. "It doesn't really exist because it has no dimensions."

"What about a singularity?" Mike asked. "They're real." JR looked confused.

"That's interesting, Mr. Castleton," said Mr. Li. "Good point." The class laughed at his joke. Since Mr. Li had not meant to make a joke he was puzzled by the laughter. "Tell the class what a singularity is, Mr. Castleton."

"A singularity is a huge amount of matter squeezed so small by its own gravity that it becomes a point – no dimensions. Singularities create black holes."

"Right," Mr. Li said. "A singularity is the closest thing we know of to a point in geometry. What is a line?"

"A line is a series of points with no ends," a girl named Tori answered.

"Right," said Mr. Li. "How many dimensions does a line have?"

"One," Tori answered. "Only length."

"If I take a bunch of lines and lay them side by side, what do I have?" Mr. Li asked.

"A plane," Nick answered.

"Right, Mr. Pope. How many dimensions in   a plane?"

"Two," Nick replied. "Length and width. No thickness."

"If I take four identical planes and I make a box, what have I created?" Mr. Li asked.

"A cube," answered a girl named Molly. "A cube has three dimensions. Length, width, and depth."

"Can you think of something with a fourth dimension?" Mr. Li asked.

"All of us and everything," Mike answered. Again the class looked puzzled.

"Explain, please," Mr. Li said, holding his hand out to Mike as an invitation to discuss his conclusion.

"Time is the fourth dimension," Mike said. "In fact, science uses the words time/space to name the four dimensions. The first three dimensions are called spatial dimensions, because they take up space. We move around in those three dimensions. The difference with time, the fourth dimension, is we move through it."

"Correction, Mr. Castleton," Mr. Li said. "We move through time in only one direction; always into the future. Also, we move at one speed, sixty seconds per minute."

"We can move in both directions," Mike said. Immediately he knew he had goofed. Only Nick knew about the Time Institute and time travel. His friend kicked Mike under the table as a warning to shut up.

"Some scientists think we may be able to travel in both directions," Mr. Li said. "I don't believe it."

"Why?" Mike asked. Again, he wished he had dropped the matter, as he knew this topic was getting risky. It was getting too close to a very important secret. Nick kicked him again.

"If time travel were possible, people from the future would be visiting us," Mr. Li answered. "We haven't met them, so I don't think they can do it. We are stuck in time, moving forward into the future at 60 seconds every minute."

Mike was glad Mr. Li didn't pursue the topic any further. He was off the hook and his ankle hurt from being kicked twice. Still, he and Nick knew their math teacher was wrong. They knew, because they had traveled both forward and backward in time.

"We have talked about four dimensions," Mr. Li continued. "Did you know that mathematics shows there may be 11 dimensions?" The students looked surprised. "Last week I read an article in Tomorrow's Science magazine about these other dimensions," the math teacher continued. "There is no proof other than in mathematics that they really exist, but they are very interesting to think about."

"What would these dimensions be like?" a girl named Maureen asked.

"No one knows," Mr. Li said. "They could be very strange. In fact, because we live in just four dimensions we probably cannot even imagine what they would be like. Just for fun, imagine a person who lives in a one-dimensional world. He couldn't imagine me as I am. If he came into our world or I went into his, how do you think he would see me?" The students all shook their heads. "He would see me as a line," Mr. Li explained. "His world could pass right through me and all he would see is the part of me that is on that line. He couldn't see anything above, below, or beside the line. Those parts of me would be in a second or a third dimension. The line that he thought was me would change color as his world went through my skin, blood, bone, and my insides. But, all he would see is a line. He would think that is what I looked like, different colors."

"Now," Mr. Li continued. "How would a person who lived in a two-dimensional world see me?"

"As a plane?" Mike guessed.

"Yes, Mr. Castleton," Mr. Li said with a big smile. "Very good."

"His world would cut through your body and he would see different colors too," Mike continued. "Maybe he could see some flat shapes."

"Yes, yes," Mr. Li said, getting excited. "You've got it. All he would be able to see of me is a very thin slice. He could not possibly understand me as I really am. Now, imagine that I move through his world. What happens?"

"He sees you change," Mike said. "If you turned or bent over he would see a different slice of you. You would seem to change shape."

"Yes," Mr. Li said. He was excited his class was able to grasp such difficult ideas. "What if his world sliced though my stomach and then I bent forward and put my arms through his world?"

"He would think you were very strange," Mike answered. "He would see you in three places at once. You would be a big patch where his world cut through your stomach, and two smaller patches where it cut through your two arms. He might think you were magical."

"I could put just my fingers into his world and he would see me in ten small places," Mr. Li said. "He could not possibly understand what I am really like. All he would know is that I keep changing. Isn't geometry fun?" he asked the class. "Without it you could never think about these things."

"What would happen if we ran into someone from an 11 dimension world?" Tori asked.

Mike answered her. "We wouldn't be able to understand what he was really like. We could only see him in our four dimensions. We could only see part of him. To us he would be really strange, like Mr. Li's fingers in a two-dimensional world."

"Exactly," Mr. Li said. "Now, let's think about another idea from that article in Tomorrow's Science. The magazine said our four-dimensional universe and a higher dimension universe could not exist together. They would have to be connected by some sort of gateway. In that place the rules of time and space might not exist, or they could be scrambled. Nothing would be the way we know it, or think it should be."

"If time and space don't work," Mike asked "Would the gateway really be a place."

"Hmmm," Mr. Li thought. "That's a good question, Mr. Castleton. What makes a place a place? A place has to have dimensions. Hmmm."

"Nowhere," a boy named Austin added. "If somewhere is not a place, it is Nowhere." The class was silent as they all pondered this.

"What would be in Nowhere?" JR asked

"Nothing," answered a girl named Emily. "If there was something, it would have dimensions."

"Excellent thinking," said Mr. Li.

Mike added another idea in the form of a question. "If the gateway is nowhere, when is it?"

"When is it?" Mr. Li asked. "What do you mean, Mr. Castleton?"

"Time works for us. We have the past, the present, and the future," Mike explained. "If time doesn't work in the gateway, what time is it?" The students all had puzzled frowns on their faces. As he thought, Mr. Li looked out the window with his hand on his chin. "I think all it leaves is Now," Mike said, answering his own question. "There is Nothing in Nowhere and it is always Now."

"Deep," said Austin. "That is real deep."

"Yeah," Tori added. "Real heavy thoughts. Wow."

The bell rang. It was 11:50, time for lunch. The class left the room still pondering the questions they had developed, "What makes a place a place and when is it in a place that is no place?" Mr. Li had a big, proud smile on his face. He wanted his students to wrestle with questions like this.

Nick and Mike found their friend Patrick Weaver in the lunch hall, sitting at a table. He had already been through the lunch line and had a full tray. Mike and Nick put their back packs on the chairs across the table from Patrick and went to get their food.

Patrick Weaver had started in preschool with Mike and Nick. The three had been best friends for 11 of their 15 years. Patrick was shorter than Mike or Nick. However, he weighed a lot more than his skinnier friends. Patrick was a short, hard pack of muscle. For years he had studied Ti Kwon Do and it had made his solid body even stronger. All the other kids respected him because of his strength. However, Patrick was a natural leader and kids would have respected him even if he was skinny.

Patrick had blue eyes and sandy colored hair. When he was in grammar school he had freckles, but they had disappeared as he had grown older.

Mike and Nick put down with their trays and sat next to Patrick. They told their friend about their geometry class and the discussion they had about different dimensions. Patrick understood, as math was his best subject. In fact, he was in the advanced math course with Mr. Li, and studied topics Mike and Nick did not even know about.

"Hey," Mike said. "I got something to show you guys, something I got for my birthday last month." He reached into his back pack and took out a small device, slightly larger than a cell phone. It looked more like an Ipod. Mike opened the device and put it on the table. "GPS," he said. "It tells you right where you are and how to get anywhere you want to go. Someday I'd like to explore the woods behind my house, all the way to Hampton Falls. It's a long way, but we wouldn't have to worry about getting lost with this."

"Aren't we little old to play at exploring an alien planet?" Patrick asked. In the second grade the boys began pretending they were astronauts and decided they wanted to become the first people on Mars. They did get to Mars first, but that was a secret. No one knew it.

"We may not play anymore, but we still like to explore," Mike added. "Don't you want to know what's way back there? We've been walking through those woods since we were kids. We got to the other side of the pond, but we never went all the way to the end of the woods. That's miles away."

"I'd rather use the GPS when I get my driver's license," Nick said. "My parents are gonna let me start taking driving lessons at the end of the year."

At that point a girl named Emma came up to the table, accompanied by two boys from their Geometry class, JR. and Austin. Emma and the two boys were freshmen representatives to the student council. "Guys," Emma said, obviously distressed. "We have bad news. The Council wanted the Sirens to play for the Homecoming Dance, but Mrs. Martin said no. She said her brother is a Dee Jay and he will bring his music. He's gonna cost us $500. That's almost all the money the student government has raised so far this year."

Patrick, Mike, and Nick had formed a band when they were 12 years old. Patrick played drums and Nick played bass. Mike was the singer and lead guitar. They called themselves the Sirens and they had played at most Atlantic Academy grammar school events. Last year, they had performed at the high school mixer dance.

"You guys would have played for free," Austin added. "We could have had live music, and it wouldn't have cost us anything."

"Instead we got some old guy with canned music, and he takes all our money," JR said. "Sorry guys. We wanted you, but she said no way. This really stinks."

The student council reps left. Before the boys could get up and return their trays Mrs. Martin arrived at their table. Mike saw the woman coming and the image of a slithering snake flashed through his mind. Mrs. Martin had been a second grade teacher at the grammar school. For some reason they never figured out, she disliked the boys and never missed a chance to make them miserable. They had hoped to get away from her clutches when they left the grammar school. However, she took the job of assistant principal at the high school, where she was in charge of discipline. She was in a perfect position to harass Patrick, Nick, and Mike.

"I saw the freshmen student council here," Mrs. Martin said with a scowl, as her eyes narrowed into angry slits. That image of the snake flashed in Mike's mind again. "I hope they gave you the news. You are not playing at the Homecoming Dance. I told you last year, you are never playing at Atlantic Academy again. My brother will bring his music to all the dances from now on." She turned abruptly and left.

"Well, there goes our career," Nick said with obvious disappointment.

"Only here at A Squared," Mike answered hopefully. A Squared was the nickname the high school students used for their school. In algebra, Atlantic Academy's initials AA mean A multiplied by itself, or A Squared. "There are lots of other places to play music," Mike continued. "We'll just have to go find them. But, I'm not giving up on the Sirens because of her."

Patrick stood and picked up his lunch tray. "I'll see you guys later at practice," he said grimly, still angry at Mrs. Martin. "Have a good afternoon."

CHAPTER FOUR
THE HOMECOMING GAME

Patrick led Mike and Nick as they jogged across the football field in their practice uniforms. On the field, Patrick separated from his friends and joined up with the other linemen. The guards and tackles were paired up to drive a heavy sled with a coach standing on it. Every time they hit the sled there was a loud thump, and the linemen yelled loudly as they struggled to push the sled with their shoulders. Nick got into line with the other line backs and the ends to practice receiving passes. In this drill two receivers would run out for a pass while Mike and the other quarterback threw to them.

The coach blew a whistle and the team gathered to line up for wind sprints. Six players got down into the stance. On the whistle, they ran as fast as they could across the field. Meanwhile, six more stepped into line, assumed the stance, and the whistle blew again. When all the players had run to the other side of the field, they started over, this time running back to where they had begun.

Next, the players lined up in rows for exercises. First they stretched, and then they did push-ups and sit-ups. Finally, the coach gave a signal for them to gather around him. "Listen up," he said. "In a couple of days all the Atlantic Academy teams will be playing the Homecoming Day games. You freshmen go first.

You kick off at 11:00. The JVs play at 1:00 and the Varsity at 3:00. The Varsity will get the biggest crowd. Most of the people watching you freshman will be your parents or the other kids in your class. Still, you will have a more spectators than any other game this year.

"You're freshmen, so you don't know a lot about Homecoming. It's a very important event. It's the day when the people who graduated from Atlantic Academy come back to visit their school. They like to look around, visit their old classrooms, and meet their old teachers and friends.

"You know the words to the school hymn, All Hail Atlantic, 'As I stand on the Atlantic shore, I think of those who have stood here before.' Well, these are those people who went here before you. They are called alumni. Some of them went here long ago and they are very old. Some graduated in the past couple of years and are still in college.

"The alumni are important to Atlantic Academy. They give the school a lot of money, and we always welcome them back. The school knows that the alumni love to see their teams win on Homecoming Day. A bunch of victories opens their checkbooks and makes them generous. That means a lot is riding on this game and we want to come out on top."

The coach put his hands behind his back and walked back and forth in front of his team. "However, we have a problem this year," he said gravely. "We're playing Poindexter Academy. Poindexter is a boarding school. They get kids from all over the country. Poindexter recruits their football players. In other words, their coaches go to other states looking for really good players. They give those kids scholarships to go to Poindexter and to play on their teams. Atlantic Academy is not a boarding school. We're a day school, and all our players are like you; you live nearby. We can't recruit. That's why Atlantic doesn't beat Poindexter very often.

"You do have an advantage over them. Their players don't know each other very well. They're freshman too, and this is their first year together at Poindexter. You guys have been friends for years. That means you're playing for your friends and your teachers, as well as for your school.

"Even though you're facing a bigger and stronger team, we're still holding some good cards. We just have to play our cards to our advantage. I have a strategy for the game. We will have to win it early. Weaver, I want to you to open the line for Pope. We have to get him free and let him get down field. He's so tall he can catch anything Castleton throws. We need to score as many times as we can before they figure out they need to cover Pope with three guys.

"Once they figure out our game plan, Pope, I'm afraid they're gonna rough you up. You're tall and fast, but you're skinny. You won't be able to take that pounding very long. I don't expect you to make it through the whole game." The team turned and looked at Nick. They knew the coach was asking him to sacrifice himself to make the alumni happy. He could get hurt real bad.

"Once Pope is out of the game, we're gonna rely on our defense to hold Poindexter and keep them from scoring. Everyone understand the plan?" The team all nodded. "Okay," the coach said "Get back to practice."

Lenore and Allie followed Jen onto the Time Institute's arrival/departure pad. The maintenance crews had moved the Auckland out of the hanger where it was ready and waiting for its crew. "When do we want to find the boys," Jen asked.

"I know just the time and place," Allie answered. "Mike told me about it last time he visited. We'll find them and we'll have a good time ourselves. I looked up the sequence and frame."

Saturday morning the Atlantic freshman team lined up on the football field. They did stretching exercises and ran some wind sprints to warm up. Meanwhile, people began to arrive and take seats in the bleachers. The players were too busy to notice three girls arrive wearing red uniforms that looked like sweat suits. The girls climbed the bleachers and sat near the top. Some people glanced at their uniforms and wondered who the girls were. But, no one was curious enough to ask.

Atlantic Academy won the coin toss. Because their game plan was to score early, Mike chose to receive. Defense would hold Poindexter after Nick had been taken out of the game. The offensive team ran onto the field. "That's Mike," Allie said pointing to the middle of the line. "He told me he's number 19."

"There's no trouble picking out Patrick and Nick," Jen added. "Patrick is the wide guy with number 27. Nick's the tall skinny one with number 8."

"He's so skinny," Lenore said in a worried voice. "I'm afraid the other team will break him in two."

"Remember our games at New Durham," Allie said to comfort Lenore. "He can catch anything."

Mike called the play. Patrick opened a hole in the Poindexter line and Nick ran through, his long legs carrying him down the field. Mike threw the pass and Nick pulled down the ball. The Poindexter player covering Nick grabbed his shirt and threw him down. Other Poindexter players piled on. The next play was a repeat of the first, but this time, Mike found Nick in the end zone. Atlantic had scored. Next, Nick caught the conversion. In minutes the score was Atlantic 8, Poindexter 0.

Poindexter received the kick off. They maintained possession until they had driven the ball to Atlantic's 20 yard line, and then kicked a field goal. The score changed to Atlantic 8, Poindexter 3.

Atlantic again received the kick off and was back on offense. Once again, Patrick opened the line for Nick and Mike threw a pass right to him. On the next snap Patrick pushed two Poindexter linemen out of the way and Nick took off down the right side of the field. Too bad for Atlantic, and too bad for Nick. Poindexter had figured out their game plan. Nick didn't notice three Poindexter players running after him. When Mike threw the ball a Poindexter player jumped and knocked it away. The other two slammed into the tall skinny player and fell on him.

"Nick," Lenore cried, jumping up from her seat. "Is he hurt?" Nick stood up slowly. There was doubt he had been hit hard. He shook his head as he jogged slowly back to the huddle. Mike tried the play one more time. Again, three Poindexter players shadowed Nick. This time they pushed him down and all three landed on him.

Mike needed a first down and called a running play. Austin carried the ball and picked up six yards. The next play, Atlantic faked a punt and Mike passed off to JR. He ran the ball for five yards and made the first down. After two more first downs gained by running, Mike decided to try Nick again. That worked. Poindexter had shifted its focus to the ground game and Nick caught the pass. The Poindexter safety tackled Nick and several other players threw themselves onto the pile. Nick got up painfully and limped his way back to the huddle. Lenore had her hands on her cheeks as she watched in dread.

Poindexter didn't make the same mistake again. Mike threw to Nick another time. The defense knocked the ball out of the air and several guys landed on Nick. This time, Nick did not get up. He lay on the field while the coach and the Atlantic Academy medic ran out to him. They bent over Nick and talked to him a long time while he lay on his back. Finally, the medic gave Nick her hand and helped him stand. He limped off the field with the medic and coach supporting him. The crowd clapped and cheered for him. Lenore cried and buried her face on Jen's shoulder. "They did that on purpose," she sobbed.

In the second quarter Poindexter scored a touchdown. An angry Patrick bent on revenge smashed through their line and blocked the point after. Still, the score was 9 to 8 Poindexter. The teams pushed back and forth, up and down the field for the third quarter and most of the fourth. There was only one minute left when Austin caught a punt and ran it back to the Poindexter 40.

Mike was standing on the sidelines in front of the bench with his offensive team. Just before he ran onto the field he heard a voice call his name. He looked into the stands and recognized the three girls in red uniforms. He was surprised, but smiled and waved. "Mike," the red headed girl called. "Remember the

Dandelions at the factory." Mike understood right away. He nodded and waved. He put on his helmet and ran out to join the rest of the offensive team waiting for him in the huddle.

First down, Mike handed off to Austin who ran for three yards. Second down JR carried the ball for another two. It was third and five. Mike called a time out. He ran to the bench and asked Nick if he had one more play in him. Nick nodded. "Let me have Nick one more time coach," Mike said. The coach looked worried but Nick convinced him he could manage. The crowd stood and cheered as Nick and Mike ran onto the field together.

In the huddle, Mike told the team the next play was not in their play books. Instead, he would describe to them what he wanted. The offense came out and formed a line. The center snapped to Mike. Austin ran across the back field and past Mike from the right. Mike gave him the ball. The Poindexter linemen saw the handoff and ran after Austin. JR came toward Austin from the left. Austin passed the ball to him. Some Poindexter players still ran after Austin. Others saw what had happened and turned to run after JR. JR ran past Mike and gave the ball back to the quarterback. Meanwhile, JR kept running like he still had the ball. The Poindexter team was split in two. Half was chasing Austin. The other half was running after JR.

Meanwhile, Patrick had run down field accompanying Nick. The players shadowing Nick stopped when they saw what was happening in the backfield and turned so they could tackle JR or Austin if one of them got past the linemen. The whole Poindexter team was confused and had left Nick wide open. Mike threw a long pass and Nick pulled it down. The tall, skinny receiver turned, and with the longest strides he could make, started running to the Atlantic end zone. The Poindexter safety saw the pass and was between Nick and the goal. Patrick was running right beside Nick protecting him. As they reached the safety Patrick plowed into him. The safety's feet left the ground and he landed on his back with his arms and legs spread out. Nick ran into the end zone and the buzzer sounded. Atlantic had squeaked out a 14-9 victory in the last seconds of the game.

The people in the bleachers jumped to their feet and cheered. Next, they ran down to the sideline to greet the team as they came off the field. Poindexter's team lined up to congratulate Atlantic, but the players were not smiling. They felt it was just plain wrong that a big, rich school like theirs should lose to a smaller school like Atlantic.

Mike waved to the girls and called them over. Nick and Patrick had not noticed the three red-uniformed time travelers sitting in the stands and were surprised when Lenore and Jen threw their arms around their necks and kissed them. Mike and Allie had already kissed and were holding hands watching. JR, Austin, and some other players walked by heading for the locker room. They carried their helmets. "Hey guys," Mike said. "Come meet Jen, Lenore, and Allie. They're the girls we told you about. They're from a school called The Institute."

The other players were curious. Lots of Atlantic girls wanted to date Mike, Nick, and Patrick, but the boys always said they had girlfriends that went to another school. The other players were never sure if this was true, or just a story. Now that they were actually with the girls, they were curious. They had known all the A Squared girls since grammar school and girls from another school were interesting.

While the team was chatting with Lenore, Jen, and Allie and asking questions, Mr. Smith and Miss Walsh arrived. They were surprised to see a third time team at Atlantic Academy, and the girls were surprised to see them. After all, Mr. Smith was Lenore's father. The two acted like they did not know each other. It would have raised a lot of questions if people at Atlantic Academy discovered Mr. Smith had a family.

Miss Walsh gestured to Mike to step away from the group to speak with her. "Mr. Castleton," his former principal said. "I understand that Mrs. Martin will not allow the Sirens to play at the Homecoming Dance tonight." Mike nodded. "You three young men will have to go home to shower and to change your clothes for the dance. I think it would be a good idea for you to bring your instruments and equipment back with you tonight.

After all, you never know what will happen. It would be a shame for the school to go without music, if at the last moment Mrs. Martin's brother was unable to come."

"Yeah, sure," Mike answered. He could not imagine what could go wrong, but he trusted Miss Walsh's advice.

CHAPTER FIVE
THE HOMECOMING DANCE

The October sun had just set and it was dark in the driveway of a small house in a small town about 20 miles from Hampton. A van was parked in the driveway, full of electronic equipment and speakers. The van belonged to Mrs. Martin's brother. He had just loaded the vehicle and had returned to lock his house. Then, he would drive to Atlantic Academy where he would play music for the Homecoming Dance. It was nice to have a sister who was an assistant principal, he thought. Thanks to her he would get paid a lot more for this gig than he could make at any other school.

While the man was locking the side door to his house a cloaked time craft landed on the lawn. Three cloaked figures walked quietly up to the van. "Are you sure this won't change any sequences?" Mrs. Alvarez asked. She was the team's S/O and she was speaking to Miss Walsh, the engineer.

"It's fine," Miss Walsh answered. "I checked the Atlantic Academy year books in the UNH library. The Sirens did play at the Homecoming Dance this year. We're not changing anything. We're making it right."

Miss Walsh opened the van's driver-side front door and reached under the dashboard. There, she did some work out of sight from the rest of her crew. "All set," she announced to Mr.

Smith and Mrs. Alvarez. "The van won't start tonight. It'll be fine again tomorrow morning, so he won't have to pay to have it fixed. Still, he's not going anywhere this evening."

"Did you know the Sirens changed the music of their time?" Mrs. Alvarez, the S/O, informed her crewmates as they returned to their craft. "I read about them when we were recruiting them for the Dr. Morley Mission. They started a new type of music called Chamber Rock. They became famous, but then just stopped playing. No one knows why, and there's little information about them in the historical record. It's a big mystery."

A short while later, students and alumni started to flow into the Atlantic Academy high school gym, a space much bigger than the grammar school gym. It also had a bigger stage and its own sound system. The sophomore class had decorated the gym with a Hawaiian theme, palm trees and grass huts. Patrick, Nick, and Mike met Jen, Lenore, and Allie outside the gym. "We were supposed to give Mrs. Martin the names and addresses of any guests who are not students at A Squared," Mike told the girls. "So, we don't have tickets for you. Cloak and wait by the side door. We'll go in and open the door like we're letting in fresh air. Come in that way."

Inside, the boys began to introduce the girls to their classmates. Meanwhile, Mike looked at the stage wondering why the music had not started. He was surprised to see the space was empty. He expected Mrs. Martin's brother would have set up by now. He scanned the gym and saw instead an angry Mrs. Martin working her way through the crowd. She was coming in their direction. "Excuse us," Mike said to his friends. "Mrs. Martin is on her way," he warned Nick and Patrick. "We need to head her off." The boys began to move towards Mrs. Martin.

"I don't know what you've done," Mrs. Martin said, her face turning red with anger. "I just know you're behind this. You wanted to play so badly you stopped my brother from coming. I will get you for this. This is not over. You three had better transfer to another school. If you don't, I'm going to make you miserable until the day you graduate. I'm going to start right now. I understand you have brought three female guests. They are not on my list. I will find them and throw them out of this dance." Mrs. Martin stomped off, looking around the gym for Jen, Lenore, and Allie.

As the boys watched Mrs. Martin elbow her way through a crowd of teenagers, the student council president came up to them. She was a senior, so they didn't know her name. "Can you help?" she asked, pleading with her eyes. "We don't have any music. This is a disaster."

"We'll make sure you have music tonight," Mike reassured her. "Find five guys to help us carry in our gear, and give us ten minutes to set up." Mike had taken Miss Walsh's advice. The instruments and equipment were in his mother's van. She had left the van in the school parking lot while she and Mr. Castleton had dinner in a nearby restaurant with Mr. and Mrs. Pope and Mr. and Mrs. Weaver.

On the way out to the van Mike found JR and Austin. He told them the Sirens were going to play tonight, after all. He explained that Mrs. Martin was furious and was looking for the three girls from the Institute. He asked his friends to keep the girls company and to prevent Mrs. Martin from finding them.

"Good evening, Atlantic Academy," Mike said into the microphone. "We are the Sirens and I'm Captain Mike. We're happy to be playing for you tonight." He wore his trademark captain's hat. His guitar hung from his shoulder by its fuzzy, hot pink strap. "Welcome to the Homecoming Dance," Mike continued. "Welcome back alumni. We honor you whenever we sing 'As I stand on the Atlantic shore, I think of those who have stood here before.' We dedicate our version of the school hymn to you." The Sirens began to play All Hail Atlantic. Part way through the hymn, they broke into the rock version they had made up in the sixth grade. The alumni all cheered at this surprise. The crowd flowed onto the gym floor and began to dance.

JR and Austin invited Jen, Allie, and Lenore to dance with them. The rest of the freshman football teamed joined them. This left Tori and the other freshmen girls jealous and pouting. They stood on the edge of the gym floor with their arms folded. They eventually figured out the situation. If they wanted to dance they had to join the boys and the new girls in the red sweat suits.

The Sirens mixed in some of their own songs with some classic Rock and Roll. The older alumni cheered as Mike duck walked across the stage like his hero Angus Young from the rock group AC/DC.

On the stage Mike was raised above the crowd. This allowed him to scan the dance floor and keep an eye on Mrs. Martin. Whenever she began to get close to the girls, he would nod to JR and Austin. The football team would crowd together and dance shoulder-to-shoulder so Mrs. Martin couldn't get through. While she worked her way around the line of students Austin and JR moved the girls to another part of the gym. Then, the rest of the team would work its way over to join them.

The freshman girls asked Austin what was happening, why the freshman boys kept moving about the dance floor as a group. He explained that Mrs. Martin wanted to throw out the girls in the red sweat suits. The Atlantic Academy freshman girls had begun to like Jen, Lenore, and Allie, so they helped the football team with their job. Now, Mrs. Martin kept running into a double wall of dancing freshman.

At intermission Mike tried to get through the crowd to Allie. He couldn't. The older alumni gathered around him and thanked him for playing music that was popular when they were young. Mike explained that while he was only 15, classic Rock and Roll was his favorite music too.

While Mike was busy with the alumni, Patrick and Nick were able to go outside for some fresh air. Jen, Lenore, and Allie joined them. Jen explained to the two boys that her crew had come to this time for a reason. Something important awaited the Fixer team at the Time Institute. She told him about finding two World War II flyers at Marrakech. She explained that Dr. Newcomb and Rabbi Cohen wanted the young Fixers to find out how the airmen had gotten there.

"We won't be able to get away tonight," Patrick explained. "Our parents are going to pick us up after the dance. Jen, you know where we hide the CT 9225, in the woods behind Mike's house. Meet us there tomorrow morning. We'll tell our folks we're going for a walk in the woods to try out Mike's new GPS."

"Tell Mike to bring Menlo with him," Allie added. "I love that dog."

When the dance ended the girls blew kisses to the boys on the stage. Then, they walked out the door and cloaked. They took the Auckland to the woods and parked their craft right next to the CT 9225. They were tired and went right to sleep. They had danced all night with an entire football team.

The next morning the girl's heard scratching at the Auckland's door. It was Menlo. He had run ahead of the boys. He remembered the Auckland and knew it meant the girls were inside. He was sitting on the craft's floor being hugged and patted when the Fixers arrived.

Jen had already told Nick and Patrick about the two Navy flyers that had popped up in Marrakech nine hundred years before World War II. She repeated the story for Mike. She explained that one the men had broken down mentally and the other was in shock. They were both being treated at the UNH Medical Center.

"We have to take the CT 9225 back to its frame of origination," Patrick said. "I guess we'll have to go back to the Institute and wait until we get to your frame."

"Don't be silly," Jen said, kissing him. "We'll all go in the Auckland. When Rabbi Cohen and Dr. Newcomb decide what you're going to do, we'll bring you back here to get the CT 9225." They all climbed in Jen's craft. Menlo jumped up on a bench and stretched out. He rolled over on his back and fell asleep with his legs in the air. Rather than disturb the dog, the boys sat on the floor, while the girls sat on the other bench.

The boys settled into their apartment at the time crew quarters. When they were cadets the three lived in the cadet dormitory. Now that they were a crew they had a furnished apartment. It was reserved for them and they lived in it whenever they were back at the Time Institute. Jen's crew shared another apartment on the same floor. The boys left their apartment door open and the girls did the same. That way, Menlo could go back and forth between living quarters. When Mike went down to invite the girls for supper he found Menlo in the living room. The dog was lying on his side with four girls sitting on the floor around him patting him and cooing to him.

Lenore's family friend Charmaine Jackson had come by to visit. Charmaine was an orphan. Her parents were part of a time team that had been killed in a crash at Roswell, New Mexico. She didn't have any other relatives, so the Smith family had taken in Charmaine to live with them. She was now a cadet and lived in the cadet dormitory, but had come by to visit Lenore. Charmaine was studying to become a Researcher S/O like Allie.

Lenore and Charmaine had grown up together. They loved each other like sisters, but they didn't look like sisters. Lenore's skin was a deep mahogany brown. Her eyes too were dark brown. She had straight, jet black hair, so smooth it reflected light. Lenore had a straight, narrow nose, just like her father.

Charmaine had wild, bushy brown hair. Her eyes were green and her skin was the color of coffee and cream. She had a wide, round nose.

At supper Jen told the boys that since they returned, she had spoken to Dr. Newcomb and Rabbi Cohen. They had asked the two crews to join them at the Medical Center in the morning to meet with the flyers. "Why don't you come along Charmaine?" Jen asked. "You're only doing simulated missions at the Institute. You might as well see what it's really like being on a time team."

The two time crews, Charmaine, Dr. Newcomb, and Rabbi Cohen walked onto the porch at the UNH Medical Center. Allie remembered this porch. When she had returned from slavery in ancient Rome she had recovered at the Medical Center. Sitting out here in a wicker rocking chair and looking at the trees, she would relax and calm her fear. It was an effective therapy and it had helped her a lot.

The two flyers were doing the same as Allie. They were staring at the trees with a faraway look. They were wearing loose hospital clothes that looked like pajamas. The clothes were covered with bizarre patterns of different colored streaks. Allie had recently read about a discovery made by the UNH Psychology Department: these patterns and colors calm patients suffering from stress and emotional problems.

"Good afternoon, Lt. Newcomb and Ensign Dubois," Jen said greeting the two airmen. "We've come to visit. We've brought some friends. These three boys are Patrick Weaver, Nick Pope, and Mike Castleton. They're another crew with their own craft. We work together a lot. This is Lenore's friend Charmaine. These gentlemen are Dr. Newcomb and Rabbi Cohen." The group all shook hands with the two men in the rocking chairs. The boys got chairs for their group and arranged them in a half circle around the flyers.

"Lt. Newcomb," Dr. Newcomb said to the pilot. "You and I have the same last name. Tell me about yourself. What is your first name?"

"I'm called Chuck, Sir," the pilot said. "My first name is Charles."

"So is mine, Lieutenant," Dr. Newcomb said with surprise. "Where are you from?"

"I was born and raised in Baltimore, Maryland, Sir," Chuck began. "I was born in 1920. Except for my time in the war, I never lived anywhere else. I'm married. My wife is going to have our first baby in six months. I joined the Navy right out of college. They made me an officer and a bomber pilot. I flew through most of the war. I plan to become a civilian pilot as soon as the Navy lets me out."

"Lieutenant, I know some of our questions will seem a bit strange," Rabbi Cohen said. "Please be patient with us. What is the date?"

"We've been here three days?" Chuck asked his friend Dubois. Dubois nodded in agreement. "So it's December 8."

"What is the year?" Rabbi Cohen asked.

"It's 1945," Chuck replied with a smile. It was like he thought the Rabbi was joking. Or, maybe the rabbi was the one who was crazy.

"What were you doing before the time team found you?"

Ensign Dubois spoke. "You keep referring to a time team' What does that mean? You're all wearing uniforms, so I'm guessing you're with the government. We've heard rumors about super weapons. Are you like the guys that invented the atomic bomb that ended the war? Are you working on some secret project? Did we get caught in a test?"

"Right now, we would prefer not to tell you too much about us," Dr. Newcomb told Ensign Dubois. "We have a big problem on our hands. The more you know, the bigger our problem gets. Do you mind if we ask you for more information? We know some of our questions may seem silly, but they are serious." The flyers nodded.

"What were you doing just before the time team found you?" Dr. Newcomb asked again.

"We were at Naval Air Station Fort Lauderdale. We had gone to look for Flight 19. They were on a training mission, but they got into trouble. We went out to Hens and Chickens Shoals to look for them. When we got there everything went crazy."

A look of horror swept over Dr. Newcomb's face. He gasped. "What is it?" Chuck asked him. "What's the matter?" The others turned to see that Dr. Newcomb was in a state of shock.

"Our problems are bigger than I thought," Dr. Newcomb replied, his face remaining white. "Lt. Newcomb, I suspect you are my seven-greats grandfather. You were lost at sea. You never returned from your mission. You and your radioman died December 5, 1945."

The whole group was shocked into silence and turned to witness the airmen's response.

"We didn't die," Ensign Dubois said. It was obvious to everyone this news had upset him and was about to cause another break down. "It's three days later and we're still alive. We didn't die!"

"Didn't you hear him, Ensign?" Chuck said to his radioman. "He says he's my great, great something grandkid. That means this isn't 1945. It's the future." He slowly shook his head in disbelief.

Mike and Allie stood up and went to a nearby computer terminal. When they returned Allie told the group, "We just looked up the Newcomb genealogy at the UNH library. Lt. Newcomb, you are Dr. Newcomb's ancestor. History lists you as 'lost at sea.' You disappeared December 5, 1945 when you flew into the Bermuda Triangle."

"That's not all," Mike added. "Your grandson was my music teacher in grammar school. Nick, Patrick, and I know him very well."

"If he's my great-great distant grandson," Chuck asked pointing at Dr. Newcomb, "How can you know my grandson? They can't be alive at the same time. Are you saying you're not from this time either?" Mike didn't answer. "That's crazy," the Lieutenant said with agitation. "It's not possible. Either you don't come from here, or you're centuries old." Chuck's body shook as he tried to understand all this. Ensign Dubois started crying again. Rabbi Cohen waved for a doctor. The doctor helped Ensign Dubois to his feet and led him back into the medical center. "Better go easy on the other one," the physician warned Dr. Newcomb. "He looks like he's about to break down too."

"What about my wife?" Chuck asked. "What about my baby? Are you saying I will never see them again?"

"I'm not saying anything," Dr. Newcomb responded gently, trying to calm down his ancestor. "We have a really big problem and I don't know what we're going to do. Lieutenant, we want to do the right thing. We want to do the right thing for you. We have to do the right thing for all the people in your family who have lived since you. We have no choice in that. We have to protect all those people."

"I don't understand," Chuck said with growing concern. "Why do you have to protect my family from me?"

Dr. Newcomb turned to Rabbi Cohen. "Jacob, can you take over? I'm too upset to keep talking."

"Because for them, you died," Rabbi Cohen answered the lieutenant. "You can't come back to life without hurting them – without hurting them a lot. I think the doctor was right," the rabbi added. "It may be best for you to rest. The situation has changed very quickly and has left us no choice. We are going to have to explain everything to you, but we can't do it right away. It is going to take a long time, and you have a lot of adjusting to do. Please give us some time to talk to each other. Then, we will come back and explain everything to you."

Outside the Medical Center Rabbi Cohen announced to the others, "We all need to meet tomorrow morning at Room 307? We have a lot to talk about. Time travel certainly does mess with your mind. Oy vay ist mir. What a mess this one is. What a colossal mess!"

CHAPTER SIX
THE PLAN

The two time teams, Charmaine, Dr. Newcomb, and Rabbi Cohen met the next morning in Room 307. Every time the boys had come to this room they had sat on one side of the table, across from the adults. This time, everyone sat around the large conference table. It was obvious, the two teachers considered the younger people equals. They were all there for the same purpose, to solve this problem.

Dr. Newcomb began the meeting by saying, "I did not sleep last night. This problem involves my family. It involves those who are alive now, but it also involves all who have lived since Lt. Newcomb was lost. This problem is so important to my family I don't trust myself to make good decisions. So, I won't be a participant in this meeting. I'm only here to listen and to represent my family. I'll try to answer any questions I can."

"I understand, Charles," Rabbi Cohen said to his friend. "This matter would be important no matter who those two flyers were. Because one of them is your ancestor, we will be extra careful. You are our dear friend and we care about you very much."

"What do you know about Lt. Newcomb," Allie asked Dr. Newcomb.

"My family has always told the story about our ancestor who disappeared. We know that right after World War II he flew into the Bermuda Triangle and was lost. His son was born a while later. He never knew his father. His mother named him Charles after his father, but she always called him Junior. Junior stayed in Baltimore. It was his son Chip who moved to New Hampshire. We have all lived here ever since. That's all I know. It was many generations ago."

"That's the second time you have mentioned the Bermuda Triangle," Jen said. "Am I the only one at this table who doesn't know what that is?"

"I have never heard of it," Allie answered. Lenore and Charmaine shook their heads, while the boys and Rabbi Cohen all nodded.

"The area was also called the Devil's Triangle, and it was a hot topic in our time," Mike said. "There were lots of books and television shows about the Triangle. It was a big mystery. The Triangle was an area over the Atlantic Ocean from Miami to Puerto Rico to Bermuda. Lots of ships and planes went into the Triangle and were never found again. They just disappeared.

"Sometimes, like with Flight 19, the ships and planes were talking on the radio when they got lost. They all described strange, but similar things. Instruments stopped working. They couldn't tell directions. They couldn't see the sun. They couldn't even tell up from down.

"There were all kinds of theories about the Triangle. Some people claimed UFOs were taking the planes and ships. Others thought they fell into mini black holes. Those are strange theories, but only something very strange could explain how such big objects like ships and planes, and so many people, could disappear without a trace."

Rabbi Cohen spoke. "The problem of ships disappearing started right after Columbus discovered the Americas. As soon as European ships began sailing through the Triangle, some of them disappeared. The disappearances went on for centuries. Many hundreds and perhaps even thousands of people were lost, never to be seen again – at least until now. No one ever knew if these people were alive or dead. Now we know that at least two of them lived."

Jen added, "Lt. Newcomb told us he and Ensign Dubois saw other people and heard voices. So, we have evidence even more people lived after being lost."

"We have a responsibility to try to save these people," Rabbi Cohen said. "They are our fellow   human beings."

"Before we start thinking about saving even more people, we should think about the problems just two of them are causing," Patrick warned.

"Patrick's right," Mike added. "What will we do with Lt. Newcomb and Ensign Dubois? If we return them to their time they change a lot of sequences. We set off Chaos. Our ethics won't let us do that."

"If we keep them here, they undergo the experience of time. They never grow older," Allie said. "We know that living forever becomes a waking nightmare. You watch generation after generation grow old and die while you live on."

"Could we take them back to a time other than their own?" Lenore asked.

"If we do that, they live until they reach their own time," Mike said. "Then, we have two Lt. Newcombs and two Ensign Duboises running around in the mid 20th century. We're supposed to fix this problem. Two of them just make the problem bigger."

"Could we put them on a desert island?" Nick asked. "Maybe we could find another planet for them?"

"Even a desert island would be discovered someday," Rabbi Cohen replied. "We have explored near space, but we never found any habitable planets."

"It looks like we don't have any time or any place that's safe for Lt. Newcomb and Ensign Dubois," Jen concluded. "They just don't fit in. They were supposed to live in their time, and nowhere else."

"We can't keep 'em, and we can't get rid of 'em," Patrick said, summing up the discussion so far. "To top it off, there may be more of people in the Triangle, and we have a responsibility to go find them. We've made really good progress this morning," he said sarcastically.

"Maybe we can't solve this problem because we don't know enough about it," Mike added. "Maybe we need to learn more. Maybe it would help if we knew how the two airmen got to Marrakech. I suggest we learn how they disappeared and where they went. Maybe we'll discover something that will help us. Jen, tell us about the two men appearing in Marrakech. What happened?"

"We were sitting on the wall that surrounded the Medina," Jen answered. "There was a festival going on and we were watching the crowd. Lt. Newcomb and Ensign Dubois just appeared in the middle of the crowd and began shouting, 'Help us. Help us.' The crowd captured them. That was it. They just appeared in the middle of the crowd. There was no warning. No noise, no flash of light. They were just there, yelling."

"So, wherever they came from connected into that market place," Mike said. "They must have passed through some kind of opening."

"Or, they were dumped there," Nick added. "Maybe they didn't get there on their own. Someone may have put them there."

"Or some force put them there," Lenore said.

"It's obvious," Mike observed. "We just don't know enough to make any decisions. We need more information, and I can only think of one way to get it."

"Yeah," Patrick agreed. "We need to follow Lt. Newcomb's plane when it flies out to rescue Flight 19. We need to know where it went and what happened to it. We need to learn how they got to Marrakech."

"They saw other people. We have to figure out who they were," Mike said. "We need to know how many of them there are."

Back at their apartment Patrick said to Jen, "We'll need you to take us to the CT 9225 and wait for us. When we finish this mission we can only take our craft to its last frame of origination, the last time we were here. You can bring us back to this frame."

"We'll take you to the CT 9225," Jen agreed. "But we're not coming back here. We're going   with you."

"No way," Patrick said with so much emphasis he almost yelled it. "You are not coming with us. This is   our mission."

"When did it become your mission?" Jen demanded in anger. When Jen got excited or agitated she spoke rapidly and slipped into her strong New Zealand accent. None of her friends could understand what she said. Allie gently gestured for her pilot to slow down. Jen took a deep breath and continued speaking with precision. "Do you remember who found Lt. Newcomb in Marrakech? You have no right to tell us we can't go."

"Yes I do," Patrick yelled. "You are not going. We'll handle this. We're Fixers. You guys are just Reasearchers. We're trained for this kinda stuff. I can't be worrying about you."

"Just researchers?" Jen yelled at Patrick, getting up into his face. Allie gestured again. Jen took another deep breath and slowed down. "Just researchers? That's an insult," she continued forcefully, but distinctly. "We had the same training you did."

Mike walked to the apartment door and closed it. He didn't want the neighbors hearing this fight. Menlo did not like his friends yelling at each other. He ran around the room licking everyone's hands, trying to make peace. Allie stooped down and held him. He was shaking.

"We're trained for danger," Patrick yelled back at Jen. He didn't back down from her. Instead, he put his face right up to hers. "This could be dangerous and I don't want to worry about you and your crew."

"You didn't mind having us with you in New Durham," Allie said.

"Yeah," Lenore added. "We faced danger there, just like you did. You didn't have to watch over us and protect us."

"If I remember correctly we all fought in the Battle at the Field," Allie said. Jen was right up front with you. She didn't run away from those blue balls. She shot right along with the rest of the archers."

"Who went with you to blow up the wormhole?" Jen asked at the top of her lungs. "I was willing to go on a suicide mission, and now you're worried about watching out for us?"

"Who piloted the Victory and helped us with that football play when we blew up the MacDonald Center?" Nick asked.

"They're not going because I said so," Patrick snapped at Nick. Mike and Nick raised their eyebrows in surprise, wondering why Patrick was being such a jerk. They trusted the Auckland's crew. The girls had proven themselves many times.

"Oh, so that's it," Jen yelled. "We can't go because you said so. What you really mean is we can't go because you're boys and we're just girls. Girls have to do what boys say, because boys are always in charge."

Patrick realized Jen had argued him into a corner and that he was being a jerk. He sat down on the couch and put his face in his hands. "Okay," he said "You forced me into to it. Jen, I don't want you to go because I don't know what we're going to find. It all sounds too weird, and I'm scared. I saw what happened to Lt. Newcomb and Ensign Dubois. These guys are tough. They fought a war where they watched their friends get shot out of the sky by the enemy. They've got nerves of steel, but now they're broken men. What they saw in the Triangle scared them and it scared them bad.

"Jen, to me you're the most important person in the world," Patrick continued looking up at the Auckland's pilot. "I don't want you to go through that." He paused as tears welled in his eyes. "I love you, Jen. I can't let anything happen to you. I couldn't handle it if something happened to you."

"I love you too, Patrick," Jen answered softly. "If anything happens to you I want to be standing at your side. How do you think I would feel if you went off on a mission and never returned? I don't want to go through the same thing that Lt. Newcomb's and Ensign Dubois' families did.

They never knew what happened to the people they loved. I don't want to spend the rest of my life wondering what happened to you. I would rather it happened to both of us."

"Jen's right," Mike said. "Nick and I feel the same way about Allie and Lenore. We want to protect them from danger and harm, but we also trust them. They're one heck of a good time team. We're safer when they're with us. They always have our backs. I remember almost being killed by a Dandelion, but Allie saved me."

"If you love someone you can't put them on a shelf to keep them safe," Allie said to Patrick. "You have to trust them."

Patrick gave in. "You're right. Of course you go with us. Right now, we all need to take a break. Let's spend the afternoon by the pool. We'll have supper together and get a good night's sleep. We can leave tomorrow." Jen sat down on the couch next to Patrick. She put her arm around his head and pulled it onto her shoulder. She stroked his hair to calm him. The other two couples kissed.

"I'm glad I have Menlo, or I'd be all alone," Charmaine said.

Everyone looked at Charmaine with shock. During the argument they had forgotten she was there. "Charmaine," Lenore said seriously. "You heard things you shouldn't know. These things are so secret we've never told anyone. Oh Charmaine, you have to promise me you'll never talk about these things. I can't tell them to my Mom and Dad. Even if you have a husband someday, you cannot tell him what you heard us say. Promise me."

"It was pretty wild talk," Charmaine answered. "Blowing up the worm hole? Blowing up the MacDonald Center? What was that all about? If I have to keep it all a secret, can you at least tell me what it all means?"

Patrick and Jen looked at each other. Then, they looked at Allie and Lenore, and Nick and Mike. "Stay for supper," Jen told Charmaine. "If you know this much, you might as well know the rest. If we tell you the whole story you'll understand why you have to keep your promise."

"You know it's impossible to go into the future, to go beyond your frame of origination. We have, and we know how human history ends," Patrick explained. "We'll have to count on you to keep our secrets, Charmaine, just like we're all going to count on each other on this next mission. So, if we're counting on you for one thing, we might as well count on you for the other. Come along with us tomorrow."

As the crews walked to the pool to relax for the afternoon Mike said to Allie, "Patrick and Jen are a couple of hotheads. I never knew that about Patrick. He's a no-nonsense team leader, and he can be stubborn. Still, I've only seen him angry once. That was when he chewed out that assistant group leader in New Durham. Even then he wasn't like this. I've never seen him lose his temper like he did with Jen."

"That's why they're team leaders," Allie replied. "Pilots have to have the math aptitude, but they also have to be leaders. That means they're strong-willed. Leaders can't keep changing their minds. When they have a plan, they have to make sure their teams do their jobs. Sometimes their stubbornness is the difference between success and failure. It could even be the difference between living and dying."

"Then, we've got two really good team leaders," Mike joked. "If those two ever got married can you imagine what it would be like around their house?"

"Yeah," Allie said squeezing Mike's hand. "But they make up with as much energy as they fight. That will always keep them together."

CHAPTER SEVEN
LOST

Lt. Newcomb flew his Avenger bomber in a straight line from Naval Air Station Fort Lauderdale until he reached Hens and Chickens Shoals. There, he passed over the Shoals and went beyond them. Then, he turned his plane around. He did not fly straight back the way he had come. Instead, he flew at an angle to his original course. He was beginning to make a zigzag pattern over the area. Lt. Fox had told Lt. Taylor to fly in a circle pattern, as that would keep Flight 19 in the area over Hens and Chickens. They would not fly off in some unknown direction, searching for their way home. Lt. Newcomb hoped that his zigzag pattern would cross Flight 19's circle route. Once the planes in the flight spotted the rescue plane, they would follow it back to Fort Lauderdale.

Lt. Newcomb heard Taylor on his radio. The man sounded scared. "This is crazy," the frightened voice said. "Everything's crazy. What's going on? This can't be."

"I'm here Taylor," Lt. Newcomb said into his radio microphone. He wanted to calm his friend by letting him know help had arrived. There was no answer, but Lt. Newcomb wasn't worried. He was pretty sure that as long as he followed his plan he would find Flight 19. Taylor's only problem was with his plane's instruments. They had stopped working. So far, Lt. Newcomb's plane was okay, and he would use his instruments to lead Flight 19 back to the air field. His goal was to have everyone home in time for supper.

At that point in Lt. Newcomb's flight, the CT 9225 and the Auckland arrived from the Time Institute. They pulled up close behind Lt. Newcomb's Avenger and followed it. The time craft were cloaked so they couldn't be seen by the pilot and his radioman. However, they would appear on radar, because time craft are only invisible to sight. Radar sees them. The time crews knew Fort Lauderdale was watching Lt. Newcomb on radar, and was using radar to look for Flight 19, but they didn't worry. According to the story Lt. Newcomb had told the Auckland's crew, his plane along with him and Ensign Dubois, was about to disappear into the Bermuda Triangle. If the plan worked, the CT 9225 and the Auckland were about to disappear with Lt. Newcomb's bomber. The mysterious radar blips following Lt. Newcomb's Avenger would become part of the legend of the Lost Flight.

The time travelers in the Auckland – Jen, Lenore, Allie, and Charmaine were wearing their uniform head covers. The crew in the CT 9225 – Patrick, Nick, and Mike – had theirs on too. Menlo, sleeping on a bench, was the only one with his head uncovered. Head covers have small radios in them. This equipment is important, as on missions, the radios allow the crew to talk to each other. They also allow one pilot to talk ship-to-ship with another pilot in a nearby time craft. Finally, the small radios in the head covers made it possible for the time crews to listen to Lt. Newcomb in the Avenger talking with Lt. Fox at Fort Lauderdale. The only thing the time travelers could not hear was what Lt. Newcomb said to Ensign Dubois. The two Navy flyers talked to each other through the plane's intercom system.

Both crews heard Lt. Newcomb tell the tower his instruments were not working. Time craft don't have instruments. They use a mental interface. This means the pilot's brain waves communicate with the craft, and tell it what to do. However, Nick had put a weight indicator in both the CT 9225 and the Auckland when he had added the superchargers. Nick checked the weight indicator. "Look," he said to Patrick. "It's gone to zero. It says there's no weight in the craft."

"Jen," Patrick radioed to the Auckland. "What's your weight indicator say?"

"It reads zero," Jen answered. "That's crazy. We have four people in this craft."

"Look at the sky," Lenore told Jen. "It's strange. It's not blue, and there are no clouds. It's just light."

"I see that too," Nick said to the Auckland's crew. "The sea is gone as well. Everything looks the same – everywhere."

"It all looks the same because everything is gone," Mike said. "There's nothing out there. No clouds. No sea. No sun. There's not even a bird. Everything is gone." Menlo heard the excitement in Mike's voice and awoke. As he looked around he sniffed the air to see if he could smell danger. He jumped down from the bench and began to pace around the craft.

"Everything's gone but the Avenger," Patrick said as he stayed directly on the plane's tail.

"Stay close," Jen said. "We don't want to lose him now."

"Look at his propeller!" Lenore said in alarm. "It stopped."

"Don't follow him, Patrick," Jen yelled to the other pilot. "His propeller has stopped. He's going down. He's going to crash. Pull up, Patrick!" Patrick didn't hear. The time crews' head covers had stopped working.

Patrick saw the Avenger's propeller stop too, and he knew what that meant. The plane would start to fall. He tried to make the CT 9225 go higher. "My craft's not responding," he yelled to Jen. "I can't climb. I can't change direction. I'm staying right on his tail no matter what I do." Jen didn't answer. "Jen," Patrick called. "Jen. Do you hear me?" There was no reply.

"Everyone," Jen yelled to her crew. "Prepare   for impact."

"Hold on!" Patrick yelled to his crew. "We're going down."

However, nothing happened. Neither the plane nor the two time craft crashed. Both the CT 9225 and the Auckland remained right in place behind the Avenger. It was like they were glued to the airplane. "Look. They've opened the canopy," Nick said. "They're gonna bailout."

"Lucky them. They can bail out," Mike said. "They have parachutes. We don't."

Both crews were stunned by what they saw next. Ensign Dubois stood up in the cockpit and put one leg on the wing. The other leg followed as he stepped out of the plane. Next, he lay on his belly and began to slide his legs over the wing's back edge.

He wiggled his feet like he was looking for the ground. Then, Ensign Dubois stood up next to the Avenger.

"The plane's not moving," Jen said to her crew.

"It's not moving," Patrick told Nick and Mike. 'That means we're not either. We're at a full stop." He pulled his remote out of his pocket to open the door. The remote's screen was blank. There was no math problem to answer.

"The remote isn't working either," Jen said to the Auckland's crew. "The door won't open."

"There's a manual release," Lenore told the pilot. "I can open the door by hand."

"Stand back, Patrick," Nick said to his pilot. "Let me get in the corner. I can release the door by hand."

The doors on both time craft opened. Jen and Patrick stepped out, pulled off their head covers, and tossed them back into their craft. "Jen," Patrick said as he saw the other pilot. "Can you hear me now?"

"Yes," Jen answered. "Where are we?"

"I don't know," Patrick answered. "Lt. Newcomb, Ensign Dubois," he called. "Where did they go?" he asked Jen. The other pilot shook her head in surprise.

Lenore and Charmaine stepped out of the Auckland, following their pilots. They too pulled off their head covers and tossed them into the Auckland. "Nick," Lenore called as the CT 9225's engineer stepped out of his craft. "Where are Jen and Patrick? They were right here."

Mike took a minute to hook Menlo's leash to his collar. "Come on, Mennie," he said to his dog. "Let's go see where we are." As he stepped out of the CT 9225 he looked over to see Allie getting out of the Auckland. He smiled at her. She smiled back and waved him a kiss. Mike bent over to straighten Menlo's collar. He looked up and he was all alone with his dog. "Allie? Allie?" he called.

No one was there. The two time craft were resting right behind the Avenger. The two flyers, the two time craft pilots, the two engineers, Charmaine, and Allie were all gone. Mike couldn't figure out where they went. They had all just arrived. They couldn't have gone far. He looked around. He could see the plane and the craft as clear as day. He just couldn't see anything, or anyone else. There was nothing but Menlo.

Mike took a step forward. He was careful because he couldn't see any ground, or a floor. Still, he was not falling. He reached down to feel the surface. His hand went below his feet. There was nothing there. He couldn't see or feel what he was standing on. Whatever it was, it seemed to only be under his feet and under Menlo's.

He took another step. It was solid. Menlo stepped along beside him and remained even with Mike. The S/O tried feeling again. His hand went below his feet this time too. He felt under Menlo. He passed his hand under the dog's feet and felt the bottom of Menlo's paw. He could feel his pads, toe nails, and fur. The only thing he couldn't feel was what was holding Menlo up. Feeling the dog's foot, Mike concluded the impossible - nothing was holding Menlo up.

Mike became scared and wrapped Menlo's leash tightly around his hand, just for safety. Right now, Menlo was the only thing that made sense. He didn't want to lose him like he had lost his friends.

"Strike the top sails!" a man's voice yelled. Mike jumped. He looked around but saw no one. Menlo heard the voice too. He also looked around and gave a low growl. Mike took some more cautious steps. He still couldn't see what held him and Menlo up.

"Up periscope," another man's voice commanded. "If we can find something we recognize we'll know where we are." Mike looked around again, but saw no one. Menlo's hackles, the strip of hair along his back, stood up as he looked for the voice too.

"Was ist los?" Mike didn't speak German, but he knew this meant "What has happened?" He looked around again for the person who had said it.

When Mike turned again to look ahead he encountered a huge wooden ship. He had been on a class trip to visit the U.S.S. Constitution in Boston harbor. The Constitution's nickname is "Old Ironsides" and it was a wooden war ship from the War of 1812. The Navy had saved the old sailing ship and turned it into a floating museum. This ship looked a lot like the Constitution. The sails were still hanging from the masts and Mike could see the ends of cannon barrels poking through openings in the sides. He recognized the British flag hanging from a pole at the back of the ship.

Mike walked up to the craft to inspect it. It was in perfect condition even though it was probably 250 years old. The paint was bright and shiny and all the brass was polished. "Hello," Mike called up to the deck. "Anyone there?" No one answered. "Hello," he called again. He spotted rope ladders hanging from the rails around the ship's deck, and realized the sailors had used those to climb down. They had probably walked off and gotten lost, just like his friends and the flyers from the Avenger.

Mike was an S/O. This means he was trained to observe and gather knowledge. This place was weird and scary, but he couldn't pass up a chance to examine this ship. He glanced up at one of the dangling rope ladders. He could jump and reach it, he thought to himself. He could pull himself up, and then climb up to the deck. No. He would have to leave Menlo, and he didn't want to risk losing his dog.

Mike walked around the ship, scanning it closely. He could see the large copper nails that held the wooden planks to the ribs. What wonderful detail. What a find. After making a tour around the huge ship Mike walked on.

"Sally. Sally. Jane. Elizabeth. Where are you?" a woman's voice called. Mike decided it was a mother calling her children. He looked around for the woman or the children, but didn't see them. When he looked back at the huge wooden ship he was stunned to find it   was gone.

"Engine room. I need more steam. What happened to the engines?" a man's voice yelled in desperation. "Full reverse. We've gotta back outta here." Mike was getting used to these voices. He knew if he looked to find the man he wouldn't see him. However, he was surprised when he heard a voice that sound like his. "Ow!" the voice yelled. "Oh man, that hurts." Then, a dog yelped.

Immediately after the voice that sounded like his, a plane appeared in front of Mike. There was no warning. It was just suddenly there. This was not a plane like the Avenger. That was a military war plane, a bomber. This was the type of plane owned and flown by ordinary people, a civilian aircraft with the wings on top. Mike had watched planes like this land at the Seaside Air Field near the beach, an important sounding name for a long, flat strip of grass. In fact, Austin's father owned a plane like this and kept it at the Air Field. He had told Mike he would take him flying someday, but Mike's mother said that would never happen. Her son was not going up in such a small plane.

The plane's cockpit door was open and there was no one inside. Mike peered into the plane. The craft was so small the Fixer S/O was able to stick in his head and shoulders and still hold Menlo's leash. A woman's purse and jacket were on the back seat, along with the log book. He picked up the book and opened to the last page. It was dated July 17, 1963. The pilot had recorded his flight plan. He and his passenger were going to Bermuda. Two days later, they would fly back to Georgia.

As he returned the log book to the seat, Mike noticed that the amount of light in the plane didn't change. His body should be blocking the light, he thought to himself, making it darker in the plane. However, it remained just as light inside as outside. Mike stepped back from the door and held his hand just over the plane's metal surface. There was no shadow. His hand should block most of the light, but there was just as much under his hand as everywhere else. He looked at his feet and discovered his body made no shadow. There was no shadow under Menlo.

Mike walked away from the plane. He wanted to look back, but was afraid if he did he would discover it was gone. That thought scared him. He had seen the plane appear. He knew the ship had vanished. He didn't like things appearing and vanishing. It was spooky. At last, he gave in to his curiosity and looked over his shoulder. Yes, the plane was gone. Mike was getting frightened. This was all too weird.

Mike heard a group of voices. They were women, but he couldn't understand what they were yelling. He thought the language might be Spanish, but he didn't know for sure. He could only tell that those women were scared, and their fear was catching. He felt a shiver run down his back, and the hair on his neck tingled. He got goose bumps on his arms.

CHAPTER EIGHT
A COMPANION

Mike finally spotted another human being. It was a woman. She was blonde and she was wearing a long dark dress that went all the way down to her ankles. The skirt part of the dress was full and puffed out, like she was wearing a big umbrella around her slender waist. The dress had big puffy sleeves. The woman's hair was pulled back into a bun on the back of her head, and she had some black lace over the bun.

The woman was walking the other direction, past Mike. She put her hands to her mouth and called something, but Mike couldn't hear any sound, even though the woman was close to him.

Mike was really frightened now. Not by the woman, but where and how she was. She was below him to his right and she was upside down. He could see a bunch of stiff white, frilly skirts under her dress. They were a petticoat, and they held the dress out like an umbrella. Mike could see the soles of the woman's high, black leather shoes. He watched her feet make each step as she walked by him.

The woman appeared upside down to Mike. However, her clothes hung just like they would if she was upright. Gravity didn't pull them up toward her shoulders, like it would if she was upside down. Mike looked at his own clothes. They were hanging like they should. Mike and the woman were upside down relative to each other. He could see her feet. If she looked at him, she could see the bottoms of his feet, and the bottoms of Menlo's paws. How could gravity pull each one's clothes downward? It would have to pull in opposite directions.

Mike was frightened. He tried to speak to the woman, but his voice squeaked. He swallowed and tried again. This time, he was able to make his voice work and he called to the woman. "Hello, Mam. Up here. No, down here." The woman didn't seem to hear him. She walked on calling silently to someone Mike couldn't see.

Mike realized that fear was getting the better of him. He took a deep breath. "I am a Time Institute science observer," he said aloud. "I am trained in science. There is nothing here for me to fear. I am a Time Institute science observer. I don't get scared by the unknown."

He took several more deep breaths. "I am a Time Institute science observer," he repeated. "I don't know what is happening. It doesn't make sense, but it can be explained. I just need more information. I will find out what is happening. Then, it will make sense. Right now, I need to stay calm and observe. I am a Time Institute science observer." As he continued to take steady, deep breaths he could feel himself relax. He was pleased. He had not given into fear and he was calm again.

Mike patted Menlo. Menlo was still looking at the woman, but he remained his usual steady self. He didn't bark, and the hair on his back didn't stand up. In fact, his tail wagged slowly. Mike was glad Menlo wasn't afraid. It helped him control his own emotions.

However, Mike only remained calm for a few more steps. A young girl appeared in front of the S/O and startled him. She had blond hair like the woman. She wore a blue dress and long white stockings. She was holding a doll. She was just above Mike's head on his left. She looked like she had been run over by a heavy machine and was squished flat.

Her face, her nose, her mouth, the doll were all flat. Mike thought the girl must have had a terrible accident.

The girl's eyes were flattened into wide circles, and seemed to stare at Mike. When she blinked, Mike realized the girl was not dead. He watched her flat arm and hand move to her flat mouth, while her mouth opened into a huge hole. It was hard to tell what the girl was doing, but Mike thought she was calling someone. He had watched the upside down woman do something very similar.

Mike spoke to the girl. "Hello," he said. "Can you see me?" The girl didn't answer, and her eyes didn't move to look at him. Mike didn't know how to get to the woman he had seen below him, but this flat girl was much closer. He could reach out and touch her, but he didn't dare. He was afraid, but still knew he had to examine this girl. Doing so, he might find some information that would help explain what was going on. "I am a Time Institute science observer," he said to give himself courage.

Mike walked in a circle so as to move around the girl. He gave a gentle tug on Menlo's leash to show the dog where he wanted to go and glanced at Menlo to make sure he was following. Menlo saw the girl too and was staring at her. He wagged his tail like he wanted to play. His mouth was open and his tongue hung out a bit.

Mike knew the meaning of the wagging tail and the expression in Menlo's eyes. Menlo had grown up with Mike and his friends. For him, young people meant adventure and play. He could get a pat from an adult, but they didn't play with him. Kids on the other hand, were fun. He was wagging his tail to welcome the girl and to invite her to play. In fact, the dog's eyes kept shifting to the doll. Mike knew Menlo was hoping she would throw her toy for him to fetch. He was surprised by the dog's reaction to the flat girl. He wasn't afraid. In fact, Menlo acted like nothing was wrong with her.

When Mike arrived alongside the girl she disappeared. He took a step back. There she was again. He stepped forward. She disappeared again. He repeated the same thing. She was there, and then she disappeared. The flat girl was different from the boat and plane. They just disappeared and didn't come back again. This girl came and went, but only as Mike moved beside her.

Mike decided to walk around behind her. There she was again. Now, he was looking at her back. Her dress had a square section of cloth that hung from her shoulders and covered some of her back. It had three thin white stripes that ran along the three edges. There were white stars in the corners. Mike knew this was to make the dress look like an old fashioned sailor's suit. He didn't know it, but this type of dress is called a pinafore.

The girl's blonde hair was twisted into long baloney curls that were as flat as her head. Her feet and high white shoes were pressed flat. While Mike looked at the girl's back he noticed Menlo had not stopped wagging his tail. He still wanted to play with the flat girl.

Mike moved around to the girl's other side. As he did, she disappeared again. This time Mike didn't stop, but returned to her front. Her huge flat mouth was still opening and closing as if she was calling someone.

As Mike stared at the girl a thought passed through his mind, something about Dr. Li and his math class. He tried to call back the thought, but it was gone. It was like when he remembered part of a dream. It came, and it went. No matter how hard he concentrated, it was gone. That bothered Mike more than all the strange things he had seen. If he could remember that thought he might get a bit closer to understanding.

The girl suddenly disappeared. When she did, Mike found himself looking at a submarine. An American flag was painted on the tower, but it was different than the flag he knew. Mike counted the stars. There were only 48. Mike remembered talking with his grandfather. When Grandpa was a boy there had only been 48 states. He told Mike he remembered when Alaska and Hawaii became states and brought the number up to 50. The flag had been changed at that time by adding two more stars. When was that, Mike asked himself? He remembered. 1959. This sub was made before 1959.

Mike walked around the sub the same way he had walked around the wooden war ship. This thing was huge. Mike had seen movies about submarines. They always looked a lot smaller on a television screen. The S/O spent a long time staring at just the propeller. It was so big.

Like on the war ship, ladders hung down from the tower. These ladders were not made of rope, like on the sailing ship. They were metal. Mike could see the upper ends of the ladders were shaped like hooks. The hooks were hung over the edge of the tower and held the ladders in place. Mike knew that the sailors had climbed down the ladders and had gotten lost, just like his friends.

Mike was looking at the ladder when he felt a strong force bump against him. It hurt and bent him over at the waist. "Ow!" he yelled. "Oh man, that hurts." Menlo yelped as the same thing happened to him. Mike straightened up. It happened again. He bent over a second time. "That hurts," he yelled. It was like someone had shoved into him. He knew no one was there to hear him. He just said it because of the pain, even though he realized it made no sense to yell at nothing. Menlo yelped again.

While Mike was being shoved and bent over in pain the submarine had disappeared. When he straightened up Menlo began pulling on his leash and wagging his tail. He wined and whimpered the way he does when he sees another dog to play with. "Heel," Mike said, tugging on the dog's leash. Menlo obeyed, but he kept whimpering. "What it is, boy?" Mike asked.

Mike spotted what had made Menlo so excited. His dog was staring at a dog sled with a full team of huskies still in harness. As Mike got close to the sled, Menlo ran up the lead dog. The two dogs touched noses and sniffed each other. The other dogs in the team saw Menlo and began to whine and wag their tails in greeting.

Mike examined the dogs. They were all healthy and well fed. It looked like they had just arrived. In fact, there was still snow on the sled runners. Mike tugged on Menlo's lead so the dog would heel. He was curious about this sled. He had read Call of the Wild in seventh grade. It was a book about a dog named Buck who was leader of a dog team in Alaska. So, Mike knew what a dog sled and a dog team were. He had gotten used to seeing boats and planes. Plenty of them sailed or flew through the Bermuda Triangle. He asked himself how a dog sled from the Arctic could get here. What was it doing in the Triangle?

The sled was covered in animal furs. Mike knew furs served as blankets and kept artic travelers warm when riding in a sled. The sled itself was made of wood and bone, and was lashed together with rawhide, a type of string cut from leather. Mike knew that dog sleds from his time were made of modern materials, like aluminum. There was nothing industrial about the sled – no metal, nails, or screws - just natural materials. That meant this sled was very old. Mike wondered if it was made before the Intuits in the Artic had met Europeans. If so, it could be hundreds of years old.

As Mike examined the sled he noticed movement at the edge of the fur blanket. It was a baby! The baby was strapped to a board and all wrapped up. Mike realized the wrapping was to keep the baby warm, but it would also keep it from moving. The baby had dark brown eyes and black hair. Mike thought it appeared Asian. He had met his math teacher's wife and their baby. The two infants looked similar.

The baby was happy, and was being very good. Mike guessed it was not hungry and must have a clean diaper. The baby looked around with its eyes and blew bubbles with its spit. The baby never looked at Mike even though he was leaning over it. He knew the baby couldn't see him.

This was a problem. Mike couldn't leave a baby behind. He didn't have any younger brothers or sisters, but he had younger cousins, and he knew babies need to be cared for. He didn't know how to care for a baby, but he knew you do not leave them to fend for themselves.

While Mike was still thinking, Menlo put his front paws on the sled and stood up to see what his master had found. The dog got excited. It was a little person. Menlo began to lap the baby's face, and the baby reacted. He or she closed its eyes and laughed. Mike was stunned. The baby had not seen him, but it could see and feel Menlo. The other people he had seen did not hear him, and he could not hear them, but he heard the baby.

Mike reached into the sled and picked up the baby; wrappings, board, and all. The baby smiled at him and cooed. Mike smiled back and said, "Hi there. How are you little one?" As Mike wondered what to do next, the sled disappeared. "That solves that," he said to his dog. "We just got a companion. I hope you know something about babies, Menlo. If you do, you know more than I."

CHAPTER NINE
KWASI

Mike continued to wander, carrying the baby, and having no idea what direction he was going. He could be walking in circles. He had no way to know, because there was nothing to guide him. He decided the best plan was to just put one foot in front of the other and keep moving.

Mike saw a man, but he was walking sideways. If Mike was standing on a floor, the man would be walking on the wall. Mike had studied the American Civil War last year, and he recognized this man as a Confederate soldier. The soldier had three large stripes on the right sleeve of his gray uniform. Mike knew what this meant. He was a sergeant.

While Mike was watching the soldier, another man ran by him and disappeared. Next, Mike saw a pilot dressed like Lt. Newcomb and Ensign Dubois. He was walking above Mike, upside down. More people appeared. There was a woman dressed in an old fashioned bathing suit. Mike had seen that type of bathing suit in old movies from the 1950s. He saw a pirate. He assumed the guy was a pirate because he was dressed like the pirates in the movies.

He was surprised to see someone dressed in a long striped robe that went down to his sandaled feet. Mike had seen robes like that in classic movies that took place in Arab countries. An Arab was out of place here, just as much as the Inuit baby he was carrying. Why would an Arab from the desert be in the Devil's Triangle?

Mike saw sailors from different countries. He also saw soldiers, and he saw people dressed in everyday clothes. They all came from different times. It was like Mike was watching a history lesson.

There was an Arab woman. She wore a long robe and her face was covered with a scarf. Mike wondered if she and the Arab man could have been passengers on a ship that got lost. Could that be how they got here? That still wouldn't explain the dog sled.

Menlo tugged on his leash. He wanted to go to the right. Mike looked but didn't see anything. "We're going straight ahead, Menlo," he told the dog. Menlo continued to pull to the right. "Menlo, heel," Mike said firmly. Menlo obeyed, placing himself on Mike's left side, but he still looked to the right. His mouth was open and his tongue hung out, like he saw something that interested him. Mike saw nothing. He had decided to keep placing one foot in front of the other, and he was not going to let Menlo's curiosity change his plan, especially if there was nothing there. "Heel," Mike said and gave the lead a gentle tug to focus Menlo's attention. It didn't work. The dog still stared to the right as they moved ahead.

Mike saw more people. At times he could see as many as fifty. They were alone and wandering in all directions. They were also in all directions – above, below, off to the side. They were in front and in back. Some seemed to be walking up invisible walls. Others had their heads towards Mike, while some had their feet towards him. No matter their position, gravity didn't pull on their clothes, or their hair.

Menlo tugged to the right again and whimpered. Mike looked again, but still didn't see anything. "No, Menlo," he said. Mike was carrying the baby, and it was still being very good. It never struggled or cried. Sometimes it would make a soft cooing sound that informed Mike it was happy and comfortable.

So far, all the people Mike had seen – and there had been lots of them – were wandering alone. Next, Mike spotted two young girls holding hands. One girl was older and taller than the other. She was maybe seven, while the other girl was about three. There was no doubt they were sisters. The girls were dressed like the flat girl he had seen. They wore blue pinafores identical to hers. Both had white stockings and white, high leather shoes. Both had blonde hair, twisted into baloney curls.

The girls looked at Mike. Other than the baby, these were the first people to act like they saw him. Menlo saw the girls and wagged his tail in greeting. "Oh look, a doggie," the smaller girl said.

"You can see me?" Mike asked.

"You can see us?" the older girl asked back.

"Yes," Mike said in excitement. "I can see you."

The girls ran up to Mike. The small girl got down on her knees and hugged Menlo. That was the only time the girls let go of each other's hands. Mike saw it happen. "Keep hold of your sister's hand," he told the little girl. Mike had just realized something important. The two girls looked surprised. "We're the only people who can see each other. You're holding hands, and I'm holding my dog's leash. That's important. It means something."

"You're holding a baby too," the seven year-old said. She stood on tip toes to see the baby's face and talked baby talk to it. The baby smiled and laughed. It didn't have any teeth, but it made a big smile.

"Yes," Mike answered. "The baby didn't see me until Menlo touched it. Menlo is my dog's name," he added. "I don't know what this means, but it looks like people who are connected or touching can see. The people who are all alone, they don't see anything. We need to stay touching, or we can get lost like they are.

"I have an idea," Mike told the girl. "Hold still. I'm going to untie the ribbon in your hair.' Mike used the ribbon to tie the girl's wrist to his. Then, he took the ribbon from the younger girl's hair and tied the sisters' wrists together. "Now, we can't become alone by accident."

Mike sat down and the girls sat with him. Mike held the baby in his lap and Menlo's leash in his other hand.

"Who are you?" Mike asked the older girl. "How did you two get here?"

"My name is Sally Stevens," the girl answered. "This is my sister Elizabeth. I don't know how we got here. I don't know where we are."

"What do you remember?" Mike continued.

"We were with Mama and Papa on Papa's ship."

"Tell me about you parents and the ship,"   Mike said.

"My Papa is a captain," Sally told Mike. "He sails ships for a big company. He took me, Elizabeth, Jane, and Mama with him."

"What was the ship?" Mike asked. "Where were you going?"

"It was the Boston," Sally told him. "We were bringing a load of farm animals from North Carolina to Florida. There were cows and pigs and sheep. There were chickens too. It was a smelly ship."

"Wait," Mike said as his mind made another connection. "Who is Jane?"

"She's our middle sister. She's five."

"Sally, Jane, and Elizabeth," Mike said thinking aloud. "I heard a woman's voice calling those names. Is your mother blonde? Does she have hair like yours?"

"Yes, Mama is very pretty."

"I've seen you mother," Mike told the girls. "She was okay. I think I've seen Jane too." He thought it might be hard for the girls if he told them Jane was as flat as a pancake.

"Who are you," Sally asked Mike. "How did you get here?"

"My name is Mike Castleton," Mike told the girls. "I'm kinda like a scientist. I came here to find out what is happening."

"Can you get us out?" Sally asked with a hopeful look.

"I'm afraid not," Mike answered. "I'm stuck just like you. How long have you been here?" he asked.

"I don't know," Sally said. "I think we just arrived. No," she said correcting herself. "I'm remembering lots of things. I've seen lots of strange people and ships. I've seen some very strange things - machines like birds with huge wings."

"Planes," Mike thought to himself. "She doesn't know what a plane is." He asked Sally, "What year is it?"

Sally thought this was a funny question. Everyone should know what year it is. You may ask what time it is, but everyone knows the year. "It's 1887," she said with a smile at Mike's ignorance.

Mike nodded. Dr. Newcomb had said ships started disappearing in the Devil's Triangle soon after Columbus discovered America. They disappeared for centuries. That explained the wooden British war ship and the Confederate soldier. A dog sled from the Arctic still didn't make sense. Neither did the people who looked like Arabs from the desert. They shouldn't be in the Triangle. How did they get lost here?

Menlo gave another tug on Mike's arm. He was looking off to the right again, like he was seeing something that interested him. "No, Menlo," Mike said. "Will you forget going that way? There's nothing. Settle down."

"Where are we?" Sally asked Mike. "Are we in Wonderland?'

"Huh?" Mike asked in surprise.

"Are we in Wonderland?" Sally asked again. "Mama read us the book Alice's Adventures in Wonderland. The book was funny, but it was scary sometimes. Wonderland was strange like this, only this place is scary all the time. I don't like it here. Alice could talk to the animals and to the people. People here don't talk. The flat people really scare me. Elizabeth doesn't like them either. I want to go back to Mama and Papa and the ship. I don't like this place."

"You've seen flat people?" Mike asked. Sally nodded. "They scare me," she said. "Why are they flat? What did that to them? It must hurt very badly."

"We should search some more," Mike said. "We won't find our way out by sitting. Remember, keep holding hands. The ribbons are just for safety." The small group stood; Menlo, Mike holding a baby, and two young sisters. Mike led the way, putting one foot in front of another. Menlo pulled off to the right again. "Heel, Menlo," Mike said.

As they walked Mike felt a string or a wire hold him back. He looked, but couldn't see it. He put out his hand and felt the wire. He pushed on it. "That's one of those wires," Sally said. "We've bumped into them before. You can't see them, they're just there. You have to go under them or around them." Mike ducked down and was able to go forward. The girls did the same. The group moved on.

"Ow," a voice yelled in pain. "Oh man, that hurts," it said. A dog yelped. Mike listened and realized it was his own voice. He had spoken those words when something had bumped him, and had bent him over double.

"We hear people yelling like that a lot," Sally told Mike.

Mike nodded. For him, this voice was different. It was his. "I'm a Time Institute science observer," he said silently to himself. "Everything can be explained. I just need more information. There's nothing to be scared about."

"Look," Sally said to Mike. "It's them again. Pretend you don't see those people."

"Who?" Mike asked. He saw a line of people coming at him. They were black skinned and were dressed in ragged clothing. They were tied together with a long chain that was connected to iron collars around their necks. Mike knew right away they were slaves. "Why would you pretend you don't see them?" Mike asked Sally.

"I'm afraid they did something bad," the blonde girl answered. "If they were good, why would they be chained like prisoners?'

"They didn't do anything bad," Mike replied. "But something very bad has been done to them. I have friends that were made slaves, and I know it's terrible."

Mike held up his hand in greeting. The man at the head of the line held up his hand in the same way. "I am a friend," the S/O said. "My name is Mike. Do you speak English?"

"Ah speak English, Massah Mahk," the man said. Mike realized the man had not been taught to speak English. Instead, he had learned it listening to the slave masters he worked for. That is why he spoke with such a strong African accent. His accent made it hard for him to say sounds like the word eye. He pronounced the sound ah. He also had trouble with the TH and the V sound. He pronounced TH like D, and V like B. "Mah

82

name is Ceasar. Dat's deh name mah Massah gib me. Dees udders, dey fresh from Africa. Dey speak no English, Massah Mahk."

"I am not your master," Mike said. "I am a friend. Please call me just Mike. I want to make you free."

"Oh, we wanna be free so bad, Mahk," the African said with emotion, tears forming in his eyes. "It is so bad being a slabe."

"I cannot call you Caesar," Mike said to the African. "That's a name you were forced to take. What was your name in Africa?"

"Ah am Kwasi," the man replied with pride. "It means Born on Sunday. Dat is deh day Ah was born."

A woman in the line said something to Kwasi in their own language. "She say, you hab a baby. Can she hold it? She hab a baby in Africa. The slabers, dey take her away. She see her baby no more. She wanna hold a baby so bad."

Mike handed the baby to Kwasi, and he passed it to the woman. Mike examined the line. There were about twenty people in it, all women, except for Kwasi. Some were just teenagers, even younger than he was. He was glad to pass on the baby. He was sure the woman knew more about caring for it than he did. The woman pressed the baby to her lips and kissed it, while the other women gathered around her to see. They said things Mike didn't understand, but he recognized the sounds. The women were talking baby talk.

"Kwasi," Mike said. "These girls are Sally and Elizabeth Stevens. They're lost too. How did you get here?

"We was on a ship from Jamaica to Bermuda," Kwasi began. "Dey sell us to a new Massah. He want all deh women 'cause dey work hard in deh fields and dey are less trouble. Den dey hab babies, and dah Massah gets more slabes. Deh ol' Massah he sell me real cheap to deh new Massah. He say Ah run away too much. Ah too much trouble, he say. Deh new Massah he tek us to his home wid deh many cows and pigs he bought   in Jamaica.

"Den, we hear deh whate men on deck. Dey real scared. Dey say evrating is strange. Dehn, dey disappear. We don't know where dey go. Dey leab us all alone."

"How long ago was that?" Mike asked Kwasi.

"Today," Mehbe a couple o' minutes ago."

"Do you know what year it is, Kwasi?" Mike asked.

The African smiled a big smile, just like Sally did when Mike asked her the   same question.

"It 1723, Mahk. You know dat. You joke wid me."

"Have you talked with anyone else here?" Mike asked.

"No," Kwasi answered. "We see many whaht people. We afraid dey make us slabes again. We stay away. We see some Arabs. Dey make slabes o' Africans too. We scared of dem like we scared of dah whaht people.

"Dey all real strange. Dey walk on walls. Dey walk on ceiling. Dey walk down below lahk dey in Hell. We see dem all flat. We do not lahk it here Mahk. We don't wanna go back to Jamaica wid Massah, but we don't wanna stay here. Dis place is no good."

Menlo pulled on his leash. He still wanted to go to the right. "Menlo. Stop." Mike ordered his dog. "What is with you?" He turned back to speak to Kwasi. "I can't take off your chains, but I have a friend who can. We need to find him," Mike said.

Menlo pulled on the leash again. Mike pulled back. "Mahk, I hunt wid mah dog," Kwasi said. "When he do dat, he see sometin'. I aways go see. He know stuff Ah don't."

"Okay," Mike agreed. "Take my hand, Kwasi. Let's go see what makes Menlo so excited." The line of people followed Menlo; Mike, two little blonde girls, and twenty chained African women, one of them carrying an Inuit baby.

CHAPTER TEN
THE DOORWAY

As they walked, Menlo became even more excited and pulled harder on his leash. "Easy," Mike told him. "Easy, Menlo. You've got people trying to follow you."

The Africans had learned to walk in step with their hands on each other's shoulders to keep their chains from jerking at their necks. Sally and Elizabeth held Mike's hand, while Kwasi held Mike's other hand, the one with the leash. "He see sometin', your dog Mahk," Kwasi said. "I know dogs lahk him. He's a huntin' dog." Kwasi was right. Menlo was a Foxhound, and Foxhounds were bred to hunt. "He found sometin'. I know how a huntin' dog act when he found sometin'."

Sure enough. Mike soon understood why Menlo kept pulling to the right. The dog had been able to see something he could not. It was an opening. It looked like a large door, large like a door on an airplane hangar. As the group walked toward it, the door got even larger, so large Mike could see sky through it. He had been wandering where there was nothing but lost people and lost craft. It was exciting to see something, even if it was just blue sky.

"Careful Mahk," Kwasi warned as they got closer. "Dis is strange. We mus' be careful." Mike did as Kwasi said. He approached very slowly and looked around with each step. At last, the group was close enough to look through the door. Along with the blue sky and clouds they saw the ocean.

"I bet this is how we got here," Mike said. "This is the opening. But if it is the opening we came in, where are the CT 9225, the Auckland, and the Avenger?"

"Dees are strange words, Mahk," Kwasi said. "I don' understan."

"My friends and I came in ships," Mike explained. "If we came through this opening, where are our ships? Where is the ship you were on? Where is the ship Elizabeth and Sally were on? Where is the dog sled?"

While Mike and Kwasi pondered these questions the scene outside changed. The sea was gone and they were looking at a grassy prairie. They could see the wind push the long grass so it moved like waves. The sky was still blue and it contained large white, billowy clouds. "Whoa," Mike said, jumping back in surprise at this sudden transformation.

"Dat's strange," Kwasi said, his eyes wide open too. Some of the woman in the line began to talk excitedly. "Mehbe we too close, Mahk," Kwasi added. He and Mike stepped back. They signaled with their hands for everyone else to move in the same direction.

About ten minutes later the scene changed again. This time there was a huge open, snowy space. Mike thought he could see for miles, and he saw nothing but snow. The sky was still there too. It was clear blue with no clouds at all. Kwasi and the Africans had never seen snow and it frightened them. "It's all right," Mike told his friend. "That's something called snow. Where I live there's lots of it. It's cold, but it's fun to play in." Kwasi turned to his group and translated. Mike could only understand when he said the word "snow." Mike guessed that coming from a tropical climate Kwasi's people didn't have a word for snow. He had to use the English word.

As Mike gazed at the wintery scene he had another realization. He guessed maybe ten minutes had passed between the grass appearing and then the snow replacing it. This was the first time since he had stepped out of the CT 9225 that he had experienced time pass. He remembered that both the girls and Kwasi were under the impression they had just arrived, while in fact, they had been wandering for hundreds of years.

Another ten minutes went by and the scene changed again. This time the small parade of people was looking at a desert. Kwasi and the other Africans chained to him had never seen a desert either. "What is dis place, Mahk?" he asked.

"It's a desert," Mike answered. "It doesn't rain here. So plants don't grow. It's just dry dirt." For the first time the wanderers saw something other than sky and water, sky and grass, or sky and snow. In the distance, Mike could see a city. He could see the wall and a gate. He saw stalls under the wall where merchants were selling their wares. "The souk," he said. He recognized the marketplace from Allie's description. "That has to be Marrakech," he decided.

He realized these changing scenes were an important discovery. They helped explain how Lt. Newcomb and Ensign Dubois had popped up in Marrakech. They must have wandered out through this doorway when it was showing the desert. It explained why he had seen lost Arabs wandering among mostly Americans and Europeans. They must have come in through this opening. The snowy scene explained how an Inuit family and a dog sled got lost.

Mike had an idea. If he could find a time craft, a pilot, and an engineer, they could leave through this opening. They would end up somewhere on earth, at some time in its history. From that place and time they could take the craft back to the Time Institute and get help.

To accomplish this plan Mike needed his friends. "I wish I could find Allie," he said aloud. Kwasi looked at him quizzically. He didn't know what this meant. Menlo had been lying down resting. He looked up at Mike too, and his ears perked up. "What did I say that got your attention?" he asked his dog. "Oh yeah. I said 'I wish I could find Allie,'" he repeated. Menlo jumped up wagging his tail and circled in excitement. He looked back the way they had come, away from the doorway.

"Menlo, could you find Allie?" Mike asked. Menlo tugged excitedly on his leash. "Kwasi," Mike said to the African. "I have an idea. I need to find my friends. I think we can escape from here."

"In mah country Ah am a hunter, Mahk," Kwasi said. "Ah am good at fahnding tings and people. Ah wan to go wid you. Ah cannot. Dis chain around mah neck."

Oh, I wish you could come too, Kwasi," Mike said. "I would feel a lot better if you were with me, but I know you have to stay. Will you take care of everyone? Keep them here? Keep them safe?"

"Ah will, Mahk. Ah promise."

"Find Allie," Mike told his dog. Menlo took off at a trot with Mike running behind him. From time to time Menlo would stop and sniff. Then, he took off again. Sometimes he zigzagged, sniffing as he went back and forth. People began to appear again. This time, Mike did not pay any attention to them. Like before, they were everywhere and in every position. He saw an occasional flat person, and he bumped into a couple of invisible strings. He heard a woman calling. He heard people cry in pain. He heard men giving commands. He ignored them all.

Another wooden boat appeared. This one was smaller than the British warship and it had nets hanging on the side. Mike guessed it was a fishing boat. He stopped to examine the vessel. He wanted a rope. If he found Allie he would tie her to him so he wouldn't lose her again. The boat had what Mike wanted. He pulled out a rope that was wrapped in a neat bundle. It was tied around the middle to keep it from coming undone and getting tangled. Mike passed his arm through the rope so he could carry it on his shoulder. He also took a knife that a missing fisherman had left stuck in the boat's rail.

Menlo waited patiently while Mike got the rope. "Find Allie," Mike said again to the dog. Like before, Menlo set off at a trot, only slowing down to sniff and zigzag. It worked. Mike saw Allie ahead. He saw her from behind, but knew it was her. How many other girls with long, auburn hair and a red Researcher uniform could there be here? "Allie! Allie!" Mike called. She didn't hear him.

Menlo was so happy to see Allie that Mike could barely keep him under control. The dog ran toward the red-haired Researcher, pulling Mike behind him. Menlo jumped up on Allie and started to kiss her, his tail wagging as fast as a tail could wag.

Allie was startled. As soon as Menlo touched her, she could see him. She took his head in her hands and gave him a kiss. She didn't have to bend over to reach the dog. Standing on his hind legs, Menlo was almost as tall as a time traveler. Mike grabbed ahold of Allie's uniform. He grabbed with such force Allie was startled again.

"Mike," she said in surprise at how roughly he had grabbed her. She had a questioning look on her face, wondering why he had been so abrupt.

He explained. "Allie, hold onto me. If we hold onto each other we can't get lost again." Allie threw her arms around Mike's neck and kissed him. "That's the idea," Mike said as he kissed her back. "Don't let go." Menlo got in on the kissing and hugging. He stood again on his rear legs and kissed both faces at the same time both faces kissed each other.

"Where's the Auckland?" Allie asked looking over her shoulder where she had last seen the craft. "Where are the others? They were just here."

"We've got so much to talk about, Allie," Mike said still holding his friend. "I've seen such weird things. They just don't make sense. I've also learned some important things. Right now, hold on to me. I'm going to tie this rope around your waist and I'll tie it around mine too. That's one of the things I've learned. As long as we're connected, we won't lose each other."

"What is that?" Allie screamed. Mike turned. Allie was pointing at a flat person who had just appeared in front them.

Mike looked too. "Nick," he cried. The person was flat, but Mike could recognize his friend. "Oh Nick, what happened?" Mike asked the flat person. He knew Nick could not hear or see him, but he knew Nick was alive. He could see his eyes blink.

Mike reached out and placed his hand on Nick. Immediately, Nick in his normal form stood before Mike, Allie, and Menlo. Mike was startled that Nick had changed so fast and easily. Still, he knew enough to grab Nick's uniform and to hold him tightly.

"Mike," Nick said. "Allie. Where are we? Where are the time craft and the others?" He looked at Mike's hand holding his uniform. "You can let go, Mike," he said, wondering why his friend was holding him.

"No, I can't let go," Mike insisted. "I would lose you again. We have to stay connected. Hold onto me while I tie this rope around your waist. We've figured out that people who are connected don't get lost. They can see each other and talk to each other."

Mike described to his friends all he had observed and discovered since they had arrived here. Allie and Nick were surprised, as they had not experienced anything. They thought they had just gotten out of the time craft. Now that they were connected to Mike, they could see people wandering and hear the voices. They believed the story Mike was telling them.

"I think I know how to get out of here," Mike said to Allie and Nick. "What I haven't figured out is where here is," Mike added.

Nick was normally very serious, but Mike's comment made him laugh. "You two brainy S/Os haven't figured this out?" he said with a big smile. "You mean it took an ordinary, hardworking engineer to solve it? I'll give you a hint, Mike. We're Nowhere. There is Nothing, and this is Now."

Mike's eyes widened. "Mr. Li's class," he said. "This is the place we were talking about. It really exists." Allie didn't understand Mike's and Nick's conversation. "Mathematicians think there may be a universe with eleven dimensions," Mike said to her. "If they're right, there's a connection between our world and that universe. There's nothing in the connection. The rules of time and space might not exist, or they might not work the same as they do for us."

"That's why we see all these weird things around us," Nick added. "People above and below us, walking upside down, and at angles. That explains the flat people. They're trapped in two dimensions. It explains the invisible strings. I'll bet those are people in one dimension."

"Nick, do you know you were flat when we found you?" Allie asked.

"No way," Nick said. "I was normal." He looked at Mike, who shook his head.

"How could I have been in two dimensions? I didn't feel any different?"

"Something pushed into me and bent me in half," Mike added. "It hurt bad. Menlo cried too. If you didn't know you were in two dimensions, I wonder if I was in one dimension, and I didn't know it. I wonder if I was ever two-dimensional and flat like you, without knowing it."

"Do you think we flip back and forth?" Nick asked.

"If we do, it looks like we may not realize we changed," Allie said. "In that case, how do we know we're three-dimensional now?" Mike and Nick didn't have an answer.

"The voices," Nick said to Mike and Allie. "I'll bet we're hearing things that were said long before we got here. Time doesn't obey the same rules in Nowhere. If something happens in here, it happens now. It stays here and now. Everything that happens in here is always happening. It doesn't go into the past, because everything is Now."

"That's why I heard my own voice twice," Mike said. "I yelled because someone ran into me when I was in one dimension. I heard my voice again because it stayed in Now. In fact, I heard myself yell in pain even before I was bumped into. My voice was trapped in Now even though for me it hadn't happened yet."

"It's possible you'll hear yourself again," Nick said. "There is only Now. You're yelling in pain now, even while we're standing here now."

"That's why Kwasi and Sally think they just got here," Mike said thinking out loud. "They did just get here. They got here now. They saw lots of things, but they were all happening now."

"Yeah," Nick said. "If you think about it too much it gets real weird. By the way, who are Sally and the other guy?" he asked, changing the subject.

"Kwasi," Mike said. "I just remembered. We need to get back. You have to pick some locks. Menlo, find Kwasi," he said. Menlo looked puzzled. "Kwasi," Mike repeated. "Find Kwasi."

Menlo didn't know Kwasi well and it took a moment for him to connect the name with the person. At last, he held his head up and sniffed. He trotted off in a direction only he knew, towing Mike, Allie, and Nick behind.

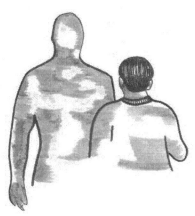

CHAPTER ELEVEN
THE BEING

It didn't take Nick long to pick the lock securing the chain around Kwasi's neck. The old lock was pretty simple and Nick was fast. Nick moved on to pick the next one, while Kwasi rubbed his neck and turned to thank Mike. As he turned Allie observed his bare back. "Kwasi, you've been whipped," she said in shocked surprise.

"Yeah, Allie," Kwasi replied. "Ah try to run away and get back to Africa. Massah whipped me. Oh, he whipped me bad. Ah hurt for a long time."

The tiny time traveler threw her arms around the taller man's waist and hugged him. "Oh Kwasi, I was whipped too by my master. I know what it is like."

"You were a slabe, Allie? But you are whaht. Whaht people are da Massahs, not da slabes."

"Yes, I was a slave once. It was long ago. I ran away too, and I was whipped, and I was branded on the face. The doctors made me better."

"Mehbe your doctors fix mah back," Kwasi said. "I would lahke to forget da whip. I would lahke to forget Massah."

"Do you hate him?" Allie asked.

Nah," Kwasi answered. "He is not worth my hate. Ah just wanna be free and forget him."

"You're a better person than I am," Allie said sadly.

While Nick was picking another lock around a woman's neck the scene changed again. The sky and ocean were back. "This is the Bermuda Triangle," Mike told Nick. "Wait a bit and you'll see some other places on earth. You'll even see Marrakech. This is what I figure, if we can find a time craft and one of our pilots, we can get out of here and back to the Institute. We can get help."

Nicked nodded his agreement as another lock fell open. The woman rubbed her neck and Nick moved on to the next lock. "How are you going to find the craft?" he asked as he worked.

"I don't know," Mike answered. "I'm guessing Menlo took me to Allie by finding her scent and following it. Time and space don't follow any rules in there, but it seems that doesn't apply to smell."

"You are right, Mahk," Kwasi added. "A dog see wid his nose much better dan wid his ahyes. Our ahyes fool us. Da dog's nose don' fool him. His nose see real good. If you wanna huntin' dog ta fahn someone, you let him smell sometin' that belongs to dat person."

"We came here in two ships, Kwasi," Mike told the African. "We had two captains. We need to find just one ship and just one captain. The captain will take us home in the ship and we can bring back help. How do we find the ship? How do I find the captains without something that belongs to them?"

"Ah don' know," Kwasi answered. He rubbed his chin as he thought. "Ah'm a hunter. Deh are tree kinds o' dogs; deh ones dat guard deh billage; deh ones dat herd deh cows; and deh hunters. Your dog, he's a hunter lahke me. I say, we go and we hunt for dem. We tie us up wid da rope, da dog, me, you, and your friens. Den, we go huntin'. When you hunt, sometimes you don' find notin'. Some time you find tings you not expectin'. We go huntin'. We see if we can find your ship and a captain. You got two good hunters wid you. Me and deh dog."

Mike turned to Nick and Allie for their opinions. They both nodded. "Okay, Kwasi. First, ask the women to take care of the baby, Elizabeth, and Sally. Tell them they must not leave this place. We'll come back for them."

Kwasi took one of the ribbons that had been in the sisters' hair. "If deh dog smell dis he will fahnd our way back to deh little girl," he explained. Next, he took the long end of Mike's rope and tied it to Menlo's collar. "Now he can run wahde," Kwasi said. "He fahnd more smells on a long rope dan on a short one."

The group of three time travelers and the African hunter set off on their hunt. They left the doorway and went back to Nowhere. Menlo trotted as far to the right as the rope would let him go. Then, he turned and trotted off as far to the left as he could go. As the group moved forward Menlo kept running from right to left. He was covering more area than they were, if it could be said that there was area in Nowhere. All the time Menlo's J shaped tail was in the air wagging. All the time he had his nose down and smelled. Sometimes he would stop. He would raise his nose high and sniff. All the time Kwasi kept encouraging the dog. "Good dog. Go fahnd it." He never said what it was, and Menlo didn't care. Kwasi's voice made him enthusiastic about finding something, anything.

The group began to see more and more lost wanderers, but Menlo didn't pay any attention to them. They began to hear the voices again. Menlo ignored these too. He was looking for an interesting smell, and wandering people and voices were not interesting to a dog on a hunt.

Menlo stopped, raised his head, and sniffed. His ears went back against his head and his tail lowered. He turned and looked at Kwasi, like he was asking a question. "What you fahnd?" Kwasi asked the dog. Menlo turned and looked ahead. Then, he turned back to look at Kwasi again.

"He fahnd sometin'," Kwasi told the time travelers. "He don' know what, but he fahnd sometin'. Get it," he said to Menlo. That was all the dog needed to hear. He trotted straight ahead while the group tied together at the other end of the rope jogged along after him.

Menlo stopped, raised his left paw, and looked straight ahead. The group saw nothing. "What is it?" Kwasi asked the dog. Menlo turned and looked at the group as if to say, "I found it. What are you going to do with it?"

"What is it?" Kwasi repeated. No one could see what was making Menlo act like he had found something. Menlo continued to stare straight ahead with his ears flat against his head. He still held his left front leg curled under his shoulder. "He say he see sometin'," Kwasi said. "I trust dah dog more dan Ah trust mah own ahyes. Dere's sometin' here."

Sure enough, a wooden sailing ship appeared in front of the group. They could see the name Mary Anne on her bow. "Dat's da slabe ship," Kwasi said. "Dat's dah ship I was on wid da women." He seemed worried that the slavers and crew might be nearby.

"Don't worry," Mike said to him. "They're all gone."

Kwasi got up close to the ship. "It still has dah cows and dah pigs. Dey waitin' for dah crew tah come back."

The ship was interesting, but it was not what they were looking for. "We still need to find one of our captains and one of our ships," Mike told Kwasi.

"Dog, fahnd it," Kwasi told Menlo. The dog understood. The people were not really interested in this ship. They wanted something else. He set off looking. He trotted to the left and then back to the right, sniffing as he went.

Menlo stopped again. Again, he stared straight ahead and lifted his left front paw. His J tail was lower, even with his back. "What you see dis tahme?" Kwasi asked. Menlo didn't move. He just stared at something only he could see.

"Do we wait to see if something appears?" Nick asked.

"Nah," Kwasi answered. "He say dere sometin' dat way. Go on dog. Fahnd it. We follah you." Menlo took off, but at a slow trot. He smelled something he did not recognize, and he was being careful. The group saw it too. It was the opening. They were back at the opening.

"Where are the others?" Allie asked.

"It looks like they wandered off," Nick said. "One of us should have stayed with them."

"Dat not dah same place," Kwasi said. "Look at the land. It's strange."

The group peered through the opening. They didn't see ocean, grass, snow, or desert. They weren't sure what they were looking at. It was like a scene on earth. There were hills and streams, but they recognized nothing else. The sun was pale blue and the sky was light pink. There were trees, but they weren't like any they knew. Some of the trees resembled huge flowers, a long tall trunk with a ball of green on top. Other trees looked like enormous feathers. There was grass, but it was soft like moss. The rocks were tall like spikes.

An animal trotted by. It had a body about the size of Menlo's. It also had four very long, thin legs and a long neck, like an ostrich's. It stopped at a tree. It stood on its rear legs and extended its long neck. It became so tall it was able to eat the green tops of the trees.

"Dere not much meat in his legs," Kwasi said. "Dey only good for soup. But Ah tink his body make some good eatin'. Ah wish Ah had my bow and arrows, eh dog. We'd bring him home tah ma family for suppah. Mah parents, dey be real proud o' der son. Mah brudders and der wives, dey only take care o' dah cows. Ah am dah hunter. Ah put dah meat in dah pot."

"Where is this?" Allie asked, wondering aloud. She knew no one in the group could answer her question.

"There you are," a voice said. Everyone jumped with surprise and fear. "I have been looking for you," the voice continued. "My calculations said you should exist. Now I have found you and proved I was right." The group jumped again as a figure appeared in front of them. The figure was like a man, but it didn't have any features. It was more like a clothing mannequin in a store window. The figure didn't glow but it had light, like the light in Nowhere.

"Who are you?" Mike asked nervously.

"Who am I?" the figure asked. "I am. That's all."

"What is your name?" Allie asked the figure.

"Name?" the figure asked back. "What is a name?"

"What do your friends call you?" Mike said. "How do they know you?"

"We know each other. Everyone knows everyone."

"Okay," Mike answered, realizing this conversation wasn't going anywhere. "You said you were looking for us. Why?"

"My calculations said four-dimensional beings should exist. I built a machine to look for you and to prove it."

"Do you come from this place?" Allie asked.

"Yes," the figure answered. "But this place is not what you see. I am not what you see."

"We do not understand," Mike said. "What are you? What is this place?"

"This is my world. I live here. However, I and my world exist in eleven dimensions. You cannot see me as I am, and you cannot see my world as it is. You see me and my world projected into four dimensions. That is all you see. There is so much more."

"Mr. Li was right," Nick whispered to Mike. "There is an eleven dimension world connected to ours by Nowhere, where there is Nothing, and it is always Now."

"Yeah," Mike answered. "We're seeing this being the way a two-dimensional being would see Mr. Li' fingers. This isn't what he's really like, but it's the only way we can see him."

"Mahk," Kwasi said in a worried tone. "Ah don' understand nottin' dat's happenin'."

"Don't be afraid," Mike said. "This is strange, but it's not dangerous."

"Dis is bery strange. Is dis a god?"

"No, he's not a god. He is like us, but he comes from another world."

"You mean lahk dah spirit world?"

"Sort of," Mike explained. "We can't see his world, but he is not a spirit. He is like us, but different."

"I want to know about you," the figure said to the group. "You live in only four dimensions. My calculations say you move only one way in time. What is that like? How do you experience it?"

"We are born. We live. We grow old and we die," Mike answered.

"Born? Old? Die?" the figure asked. "Please explain."

"This isn't going to be easy," Mike said to the figure. "Guys," he said to his friends. "I could use a little help here."

"Our bodies come into existence. As we move through time our bodies do not work as well as they once did," Allie said. "That is called growing old. Then, our bodies stop working. That is called death. All four-dimensional creatures do this."

"If you were not, how can you become? If you are, how can you no longer be?" the figure asked with surprise. "What happens to you when you die?"

"We don't know," Allie answered. "The people who are still living bury our bodies in the ground. Many say we continue to live, but in another form. They say death leads to happiness. Some say that after death we no longer exist."

"How could someone who exists not exist?" the figure asked.

"We can't answer that," Mike said. "The question is a puzzle for us, just as it is for you."

"You said you built a machine to find us," Nick said. "Can you tell me about it?"

"The machine creates a four-dimensional pulse," the figure said. "The pulse is a signal. It moves back and forth and it repeats over and over. I hoped four-dimensional beings would detect the signal and search to find where it was coming from. When they came to a place where I could contact them, I would use the machine to project myself into four dimensions. It worked. You got my signal.

"I am sorry that I cannot stay" the being continued. "The machine only projects me for a short while, and it is weakening. I will come back to talk with you again."

The figure disappeared, but the group remained to examine this new world. Birds flew in the pink sky and insects buzzed about. They couldn't see the bugs, as they moved too quickly, but they watched more strange animals come and go. Kwasi led them to a stream. Water flowed in it. Water. This was the same in both worlds. Cold, fresh water. Kwasi got down on his belly and looked into the stream where he saw fish. "Dog," he said to Menlo. "Ah wish Ah had my bow and arrows. Dem fish would make a good suppah. Ah'd trow you dah heads and dah bones to eat. We'd share dah food we catch, you and me." Menlo stood next to Kwasi and stared down into the stream, where he saw the fish too. He wagged his tail in excitement.

"Dis is a good place, Mahk," Kwasi said. "Der is lots o' food here." Kwasi reached quickly into the stream and flipped a fish onto the bank. "Der you are, dog. Hab your dinnah." Menlo seized the fish in his mouth. He lay down on the grass and began to eat it.

"This has been an important discovery," Mike told Kwasi and the others. "But we're hunting for a time craft and a captain. We need to keep looking."

CHAPTER TWELVE
TIME PASSES

The group exited the new world through the doorway and returned to Nowhere. There, Menlo continued his back and forth hunting trot with his nose down and sniffing. Once again he stopped and looked straight ahead. His ears were against his head and his J tail was straight with his back. It wagged in excitement. "What you find dis tahme?" Kwasi asked Menlo. "You wag your tail. Dat mean you know what you found. What it is it?" Menlo turned and looked at his friends. He was saying he had done his job, and it was their turn to do theirs.

An object appeared. Kwasi was surprised, but everybody else knew what it was. The name Auckland on the front identified the time craft. "This is one of our ships," Allie said to Kwasi with excitement. "This is my ship. I'm one of its crew." Kwasi understood.

"It is a strange ship," he said.

"This is good," Mike added. "We're one step closer to getting help. Now, we need a pilot." Kwasi did not know the word pilot. "The ship's captain is called a pilot," Mike explained. "If we find one of our pilots, we can go for help."

"Gib da dog sometin' dat belong to dat pahlot and he find dat person for you,"   Kwasi answered.

"There must be something in the Auckland with Jen's scent," Mike said to Allie. Allie jumped in and came out holding Jen's head cover. "This should do it," she said as she gave the cover to Kwasi.

Next, each person lifted one corner of the time craft. They had no choice. They had to take it with them, or they would lose it again. Kwasi held the head cover down for Menlo to sniff and the dog immediately knew his next assignment. He knew he was supposed to find Jen.

Menlo recommenced his back and forth trot, slowing only to lift his nose and sniff. This time his tail was wagging rapidly and there was excitement in his step. He changed course and began to run. For a Foxhound, the hunt begins when he finds the scent. For him, this is the fun part. Menlo dragged the group of people behind him. They were carrying a time craft and could not move as fast as the dog. They had to hold him back. Menlo began to bay. Baying is the type of bark that hounds make. It is like a yodel. Aroooo-rooo-roo. Aroooo-rooo-roo Aroooo-rooo-roo.

The group located Jen in a group of people all wandering in different directions. Her Red Researcher uniform and her short dark hair were easy to spot. She was turning her head side-to-side as she walked, like she was looking for something. There was a problem. Jen was not on the same level as the group. She was walking above them. They could see the soles of her uniform slippers. "You are tall, Nick," Kwasi said. "Fast. Climb up on mah shoulders. You grab her foot."

Kwasi stooped down and Mike helped Nick get on his shoulders. Meanwhile, Allie held onto the Auckland to make sure it did not get lost. Kwasi stood up, while Mike helped Nick keep his balance and stand up too. Nick's long body and long arms were enough. He reached up as Jen walked past and grabbed her foot. As soon as he did Jen saw him. Nick was surprised that he was able to easily pull Jen down to his height. It was like pulling down a balloon on a string. When she was low enough, Mike took her other foot while Nick climbed down. "Hold on, Jen," Mike said. "I need to tie this rope around your waist. Then we can explain everything."

Mike began to describe Nowhere to Jen. "Of course," she said before he had gotten very far. "I've read about this.

Mathematicians think there may be a connector between our four-dimensional world and a world of eleven dimensions."

"How did you know about this," Mike asked, a bit disappointed. He wanted to tell her what he had figured out.

"I'm a time craft pilot," Jen answered. "We all love math. I've read about this connector in math magazines. You can bet Patrick has too. So, we have finally found it. This will make a lot of mathematicians happy." She was sorry she didn't get to see the eleven-dimensional world, but Nowhere was interesting enough. There were lots of curious things to see, now that she was tied to the others.

"We think we can get out of here," Allie said to Jen. "Mike has a plan. Let's get back. He can explain it to you while we find the doorway." Kwasi let Menlo sniff Sally's ribbon and Menlo understood what he was supposed to do. Find the little girl. He took off at a trot, weaving back and forth as far as the rope would let him. All the time he was sniffing.

Again, Menlo stopped. He looked straight ahead with his paw lifted. His tail was straight up in the air and wagging. "Dat means he fahnd somethin' he already know," Kwasi said, reading the dog's silent message. "If dah dog know it, you know it, Mahk."

Once again, Menlo had found something before it appeared. When it did appear, it was Charmaine in two dimensions. Mike knew exactly what to do. "Jen, would you like to do the honors?" he asked. "Just touch her and immediately grab her so she doesn't disappear again. While you hold her, I'll tie our rope to her."

Charmaine was happy to be back with her friends. She hugged each one, working her way from the back of the rope to the front. She was surprised when she came to Kwasi. Jen and Allie recognized the look in her eyes. She liked what she saw and wanted to get to know this guy. "This is Kwasi," Allie said to Charmaine. "Kwasi, Charmaine is a member of our crew."

Charmaine gave Kwasi her hand to shake. "Pleasure to meet you," she said. Kwasi wasn't sure what to do. As a slave he would never dream of touching a woman who wasn't a slave. He would have been whipped again. Allie had been a slave and she understood his hesitation. "It's okay, Kwasi. You can shake her hand. You're a free man now. Remember how you were before you were a slave. Be that man again. Be free." Kwasi smiled in happiness. He had been a slave so long he had forgotten how to think like a free man. He smiled as he realized he didn't have to take orders, or fear anyone anymore.

The group picked up the Auckland. Six people were carrying the lightweight craft, so no one was doing any hard work. Charmaine was on a rear corner with Kwasi on the front corner ahead of her. Allie was on the other rear corner, and Jen was in between them. Charmaine watched Kwasi while he walked. He was strong. She could see every one of the muscles in his back. His dark skin was shiny. She turned to Allie and mouthed, "He's gorgeous." Allie nodded in agreement. She had thought the same thoughts. Jen bent her arm like a weightlifter showing his arm muscles. The gesture said to Charmaine and Allie that Jen had checked out Kwasi too. The other two girls nodded; he was strong, and he was handsome.

Menlo led the group through a crowd of people who were wandering in all different directions and at all angles. Voices without bodies kept calling. Because Mike, Nick, and Kwasi were carrying the front of the craft they could see where the group was going. They were the first to see the doorway, while the girls only heard it. Man, did they hear it! The baby was crying, and it was crying loudly. Elizabeth was crying too, and Sally didn't look happy.

One of the women saw the group arrive. She got up and ran to Kwasi speaking to him in their language. "She say dah baby need to be changed. It is hungry and wanna eat. She say dey all hungry and tirsty."

The group put down the craft. It was safe now that they were in the doorway. Just in case, Nick and Jen kept their hands on it. That is an engineer's and a pilot's first thought - always protect and care for the craft.

Allie made immediate sense of the new situation. "Sure," she said to Mike. "We should have known this would happen. As long as everyone was in Nowhere, they stayed in Now. The baby was happy and dry when the dog sled went in. So, it stayed happy and dry. Here in the doorway, spatial dimensions and time follow the rules of our world. Time passes, so someone waiting in the doorway will get hungry and thirsty."

"We have a problem," Mike said to the others. He said it so they would know he was asking for advice. "We have to feed these people and get them water. We need to feed the baby and get it changed. We can't just run down to the market for food and diapers."

"Der's lots a food and watah in dat udder place, Mahk," Kwasi said. "You and your friends need to go for help in your ship. Leave deh dog wid me. Ah take dees women and deh baby back to deh udder place. Dah dog and me, we will hunt food for dem. In Africa we use dry plants to cover deh babies. Dah women will find plants like dah ones we use. We will wait for you in deh udder place. Everyone will be safe wid me and dah dog. Dey will hab full bellies."

Mike really wished Patrick was here to make this decision. Being in charge was harder than it seemed. He smiled. He had just remembered, Jen was a pilot. She should be in charge. "Jen, you're the pilot and this is your craft. You're in command. What do we do?"

"I'm new to all this," Jen said. "You've been tied to Menlo since you got here. You've seen more than I have. Allie, Nick, you've been to that other world. Give me your advice."

"There was a lot of food and water," Allie said. "We watched Kwasi pull a fish out of a stream with his hand."

"We didn't see any danger there," Nick added. "Even so, Kwasi can handle himself."

"Then we agree," Jen decided. "Kwasi, we'll go for help. Take Menlo, the women, the girls, and the baby. Go back to the other world and wait for us. Don't wander. Stay by the stream. We'll find you there."

Kwasi nodded. Each time traveler untied the rope around his or her waist and Kwasi then tied it around the women's waists. In the middle of the line of women he tied Sally and Elizabeth. One of the women carried the baby. "I'll go too," Charmaine offered. Her friends were surprised. "I'm just a cadet," she explained. "On the Auckland, I'd be in the way. You're all fully trained, with lots of experience. I can't help you, but I can help Kwasi with the women and the children."

Jen looked at the rest of the crew, asking for their opinions. No one had any problems with Charmaine's idea. "Okay, Charmaine. Go with Kwasi," she said.

"What about Patrick and Lenore?" Nick asked.

"Menlo can't be in two places at once," Mike replied. "He can't take Kwasi and the women to the other world and also look for Patrick and Lenore. He has to do one or the other. Patrick and Lenore are safe. They're wandering, but they aren't in any danger. The baby, the girls, the women; they're hungry and thirsty. In my mind they come first." Nick shrugged in agreement.

"Dog, find deh udder world," Kwasi told Menlo. Menlo turned and looked at Mike like he was asking for permission.

"It's okay, Mennie," Mike told the dog. "I'll be back in a bit. Go with Kwasi. Be a good boy and take good care of everyone." Permission was all Menlo needed. He trotted off while Kwasi held the rope, which was also connected to a long line of people. They made a strange looking parade.

"Charmaine is clever," Jen said to Allie. "We're going to work. She gets to hang out with that hunk."

"Yeah," Allie agreed. "I'm sorry I didn't think of it. Don't you just want to squeeze those muscles?"

"What are you two talking about?" Mike asked.

"It's Kwasi," Allie answered. "He's gorgeous. Don't you know that's why Charmaine asked to go with him? She's got a crush on him."

"I don't think he's that good looking," Mike said, a bit jealous. "And I'd rather you were looking at me."

Allie laughed and hugged him. "I love you, Mike. But, Kwasi, where have you been all my life? You take a girl's breath away."

The crew climbed into the Auckland. "Time Institute," Jen said. "Here we come."

CHAPTER THIRTEEN
THE SIGNAL

The Auckland reappeared on the Time Institute's arrival/departure pad. It was still morning. Jen led Mike, Nick, and Allie straight to the MacDonald Center. "Can you ask Dr. Newcomb and Rabbi Cohen to meet us at the UNH Medical Center at 1:00?" Jen asked Dr. Newcomb's assistant, Mr. Takahashi. The man nodded and said he would pass on the message.

The group met the teachers in the medical center's lobby. "We've got a lot to tell you," Jen said to the two adults. "We asked you to meet us here because Lt. Newcomb and Ensign Dubois need to know what we've found out. They need to know that they are not crazy. They only saw some crazy things, things we've seen too."

Just like last time, the group found the two flyers out on the porch sitting in rocking chairs. They pulled up chairs for themselves and placed them in a half circle around the two men. "Lieutenant, Ensign," Jen began. "We have a good idea of what happened to you. We're going to tell you about it in hopes the knowledge will help you get better. You did not imagine what you saw. You are not crazy."

She turned to Mike. "Will you explain? You saw a lot more than rest of us."

Mike nodded. "I don't know what mathematicians were theorizing in 1945," he began. "So, some of this may seem really strange. We live in three dimensions – height, length, and depth. These are called spatial dimensions because they take up space. Time is a fourth dimension. Back in the early 21st century mathematicians were attempting to understand the whole universe and they used math to figure out what was happening in places they couldn't see. Those places could be really big like galaxies, or really small like atoms. Their math only made sense if there were eleven dimensions. So, they came to think there must be seven more dimensions than we experience."

Jen added, "Mathematicians in my time all agree. They still believe there are eleven dimensions, but there is no way to prove it. They think other worlds exist in those other dimensions and these worlds could even be right next to ours. We just don't know."

"Well, we know now," Mike continued. "Calculations told mathematicians that four-dimensional worlds and eleven-dimensional worlds could be connected. Think of a hallway between two worlds. In that hallway the laws of time and space don't exist. Or, they don't work the way we know them. Gentlemen, we have all been in that hallway."

Lt. Newcomb and Ensign Dubois looked like they didn't believe Mike's explanation. "Do you expect us to swallow this?" Lt. Newcomb asked. "I still think you all work for the government, and we got caught in some sort of experiment. You're not gonna let us go because what we saw is a big secret, and we might talk. You're trying to confuse us. You want us to think we got caught in some sort of science fiction world instead."

"Let me describe what happened to us," Mike answered. "If we start at the beginning it may help you to believe. I will tell you exactly what you saw. We followed your Avenger bomber when you flew over Hens and Chickens Shoals. There were two time craft right on your tail. We were cloaked so we were invisible. You couldn't see us."

Lt. Newcomb's eyes opened wide as he remembered the radio message from Air Station Fort Lauderdale. "You're lying," he said to Mike. "The radar man said he saw three craft. If you're gonna try to pull a fast one on Dubois and me, you need to get your facts straight."

Mike was the one to be surprised. He had been there, and there were only two craft. Perhaps Lt. Newcomb's memory was wrong. The flyer had been through a lot since he entered the Devil's Triangle. "We saw your propeller stop," Mike continued. "We were afraid you were going to crash. We tried to pull up and fly over the Avenger, but we couldn't. We were afraid we were going to crash too. We watched Ensign Dubois open the canopy. We saw him stand up and step onto the wing. We saw him lie on his stomach and feel around with his foot. Lt. Newcomb, we watched you get out and stand beside him. Ensign Dubois, we saw you take hold of Lt. Newcomb's parachute strap. It's a good thing you did. If you hadn't, you both would still be lost in the hallway between worlds."

The two flyers listened. Mike knew all the details, just as they had happened. Was it possible he really was there? They still weren't sure. "Go on," Lt. Newcomb said. "What happened next?"

"You disappeared," Mike said. "Your plane disappeared too. We got out of our time craft, and each one of us disappeared and got lost. I don't know exactly what you saw, but I saw some of the same things. You see, I had my dog on a leash. In this place a person alone sees nothing. They just wander without knowing it and remain doing what they were doing when they disappeared. If you're tied to, or touching someone else, you can see and hear all those people lost in there.

"I found two little girls holding hands. I found a group of African slaves. We could see and talk to each other because we were all connected to someone else. I left those people in there. They're safe. They have a man with them named Kwasi. He's taking care of all the people we've rescued so far. He's a good man and he's been a lot of help.

"Lieutenant, Ensign, you saw the people in there, but they couldn't see you," Mike continued. "You saw them at angles.

You saw them above you and below you. All of them were just wandering. There were people in two dimensions. You saw them flattened out like pancakes. You ran into invisible wires. These were people in just one dimension. You saw ships and airplanes from all different time periods. I saw a wooden warship. I saw a submarine. You heard voices," Mike continued. "Sometimes you understood them. Sometimes they were in other languages."

The two flyers listened closely. "Yeah, we saw all those things," Lt. Newcomb said. It was possible Mike was telling the truth. He had seen everything they had seen. They were beginning to believe him.

"We had to give the place a name so we could talk about it," Mike explained. "We call it Nowhere, because that's what it is. It's a place without spatial dimensions and without time. It doesn't have what makes a place a place.

"Did you notice that you never saw anything other than the wandering people and their ships or planes? In Nowhere there is Nothing. There is light, but it doesn't come from anywhere. It's just there. It's everywhere. There are no shadows.

"The people you saw, they were doing the same things they were doing when they got lost. That's because there is no time. Time doesn't pass. There is only Now. People go on doing what they were doing when they got lost, because nothing changes in Nowhere.

Lt. Newcomb and Ensign Dubois nodded. This was weird and could still be a lie, but Mike was making sense out of what they had seen.

"We saw all the same things you did," Mike said. "We also explored and we learned some important things. The opening we all went through keeps changing places. Sometimes it's over the Atlantic Ocean in the area we call the Bermuda Triangle. We also saw it shift to an Arctic area that is all snow. We saw a grassy prairie. We saw the desert outside Marrakech.

"When the doorway is open people sometimes wander in and get lost. We found an Inuit dog sled with a baby girl still in it. Her parents had stepped off the sled and got lost. We saw some Arab men and women. They must have been coming or going to Marrakech.

"You two were lucky," Mike told the flyers. "Lots of people wandered into Nowhere. You actually wandered out. It's a good thing you exited at Marrakech, because if you had wandered out into the Triangle you would have been lost at sea. If you had wandered out into the Arctic you would have frozen to death.

"If someone's unlucky, and in the wrong spot when the doorway opens, he gets lost. Most people in Nowhere came in through the opening when it switched to the Triangle. That's because lots of planes and ships pass through that area. There aren't a lot of people on the prairie, in the desert, or in the arctic. This has been happening for a long time, probably since America was discovered. That's why the ships and planes in there come from all different time periods."

"Yeah. We saw people from different times and places," Ensign Dubois added. "I thought they were ghosts because they didn't see us."

Mike continued. "We don't know why the doorway to Nowhere keeps opening, and why it opens in different places on earth. We don't know why things in Nowhere keep appearing and disappearing. It's sort of like a kaleidoscope in there. That's a toy kids play with. You look through a kaleidoscope and you see a pattern of colors. Every time you turn the tube the pattern changes. That's similar to what happens in Nowhere. The stuff you see keeps changing. It's there one second and it's gone the next. You'll see a group of people. They disappear and then, another group is there. People shift between three, two, and one dimensions." The flyers nodded. They had been there and seen all this. Dr. Newcomb and Rabbi Cohen looked amazed.

"It gets weirder," Mike warned the flyers, as well as the two teachers. "We found another doorway. It opens into an eleven-dimensional world. We went in. The sky was pink and the sun was blue. The place was full of life. We saw plants, birds, and animals. My dog ate a fish. We met a being from that world and talked with him."

"What did he look like?" Rabbi Cohen asked.

"He was just a figure," Mike explained. "He didn't have any features. He was like a clothes dummy in a store window. He glowed, but he didn't give off any light. We know this is not what he's really like. It's is only how he appears to us in four dimensions."

"What did he say to you?" Dr. Newcomb asked.

"It was difficult to talk to him. He doesn't understand a lot of things that are normal to us. He couldn't understand what a name is. All the others like him just know each other. He wanted to know what it was like to live in time that only moves into the future. He couldn't understand being born, growing old, or dying. For him I'm guessing time moves both ways, so he and the others like him don't change. They live forever.

"He's curious and he has been looking for us. He said his calculations showed that four-dimensional beings should exist. His goal was to find some of us and prove he was right. He must be a kind of scientist. He told us he built a machine that sends out a signal that repeats over and over. He said it was a signal that we could see, or detect. He hoped we would be attracted to the signal. Then, he could speak to us by projecting himself into four dimensions.

"For some reason he can't stay that way long. He had to go, but told us he would come back to talk to us again."

Mike looked at the flyers and the teachers. They were stunned. He glanced at Nick and recognized the look on his friend's face. He had seen it before, whenever Nick had a really brilliant idea. "What's up?" Mike asked him.

"The being told us sends out a repeating signal," Nick said. "We saw a repeating change in the opening – the Triangle, Marrakech, the Artic, the prairie. We saw the repeated scrambling of the people in Nowhere. I don't think this is an accident. I'm betting this guy is causing all these things. At least his machine is. I'll bet every time his signal repeats, the opening changes. Everyone and everything in Nowhere scrambles. It's his machine. It's doing it." Nick didn't usually get excited, but he was excited now as important parts of the puzzle came together in his mind.

"We can close the door so no one else gets lost. All we have to do is tell him he is hurting people in four dimensions. He has found what he wanted to prove. Now, he needs to shut off his machine and not run it again."

"It sounds like that would work, if we can get him to stop," Jen answered. "I didn't talk to him. Did he sound like he would care that he was hurting us?"

"Hard to say," Mike replied. "He had trouble understanding what makes us tick. The only thing we can do is to wait until he shows up again and ask him."

CHAPTER FOURTEEN
BAD NEWS

"That brings us to our next problem," Mike told the group – the two flyers, the two teachers, Nick, Allie, and Jen. "Even if we can get the eleven dimension guy to shut off his machine, what do we do with all the people stuck in Nowhere? We can't leave them there. There are hundreds of them, maybe even thousands - men, women, and children from all time periods. We have to save them. Then, we have to figure out what to do with them."

"We've been through this before," Nick said. "We can't take them back to their times. We can't bring them back here. There's no place we can take them where they don't create really big problems."

"What are you talking about?" Lt. Newcomb asked with a worried look. "What do you mean you can't take us back to our time? I want to go back to my wife. She's gonna have a baby. I know from Dr. Newcomb here that my baby's gonna be a boy. I want to know my son. You don't have any right to decide what happens to me and Dubois. Take us home. As for the others, take them home too. That's where they belong."

Mike looked at the adults for help. Chuck continued arguing. "He's not from this time," he said accusingly, pointing at Mike. "He can come and go. Why can't we?"

"Lieutenant," Dr. Newcomb said to his ancestor. "You're my grandfather. I care very much about you, but I also care for my entire family. You disappeared, but their lives went on. We're time travelers. We know that if we change the past even a little bit, we set off a terrifying phenomenon we call Chaos. We damage a lot of lives.

"Let me give you an example," Dr. Newcomb offered. "If you go back to your time and bring up your son, what do you want for him? How would you raise him?"

"I'd teach him to play baseball," Lt. Newcomb answered. "My dream is that he pitches for the Baltimore Orioles. I want him to win the World Series."

"I know our family history," Dr. Newcomb said. "I know what Junior Newcomb did with his life. After you disappeared, your wife lived alone with Junior for several years. She couldn't accept that you were gone. She loved you with all her heart.

"In time, she met a lawyer and married him. Her new husband was a good man. He raised Junior as if he was his own son. Junior became a lawyer, just like his stepdad. He became a special type of lawyer. He worked in civil rights. During the 1970s he helped the president and Civil Rights leaders to write civil rights laws. Those laws protected millions of African Americans and helped end discrimination. Millions of people benefited from Junior's work. He changed countless lives for the good.

"Junior Newcomb was a fine man. He spent his life helping others. You should be very proud of your son. I'm certainly proud that he was my grandfather. However, if you go back and raise Junior differently, he will never become that man. His work will not get done, and millions of people will be hurt. Would it be worth all that in order to play for the Orioles?"

Lt. Newcomb was silent, with a look of horror on his face. After a while he burst into tears. "I want to be with my wife. I want to raise my son," he said between sobs. "This isn't fair." He cried some more. "I'm so close. It would be so easy for you to take me back." He continued to cry. Then he blurted, "You're right. It wouldn't be fair for me to change Junior's life. Oh, this hurts so much. It is so hard."

"Ensign," Dr. Newcomb said turning to the other flyer. "You weren't married. So, you didn't leave a wife and children behind, but you left your parents and your brother. In your memory they started a program that brought war orphans to the United States. They arranged adoptions for hundreds of these children. Those young people had better lives, in memory of you.

"These orphans went on to have families of their own. Their children were Americans and were good citizens. Those children worked hard and raised their own kids. Their families are still with us today and are still working to make the world a better place. If you go back, none of that happens. All those orphans your family rescued, they go on living miserable lives in countries that were destroyed by war."

Ensign Dubois had the same look on his face as Lt. Newcomb. He put his hand over his mouth and slowly shook his head. It was too much to understand. It hurt so much to think he would never see his parents and brother again.

Dr. Newcomb and Rabbi Cohen were equally distressed. The young time travelers all had tears in their eyes. They could tell how much this realization hurt the two flyers. Mike felt awful. He remembered feeling this way before. When was it? Oh, yeah. It was in Hilton, the little town in England. He, along with Nick and Patrick, had to tell Tom Littlefield's wife and children that Tom had died at Agincourt. Now, he was telling two flyers they had to let their families think they had died. "This is even worse than Hilton," he thought to himself. "Compared to these two guys, Tom was lucky. He felt nothing. Only his family suffered. Now, both these guys and their families have to suffer. Sometimes I really hate this job. Time travel messes with your mind, and it's no fun."

Lt. Newcomb looked up suddenly with horror on his face. "Dubois and I. We're a problem for you," he said in alarm. "You said you haven't got any place to put us. You wouldn't kill us to get rid of us, would you?"

Rabbi Cohen and Dr. Newcomb were equally horrified. "Of course not! What would make you think that thought?" the rabbi asked in startled amazement.

"Dubois and I just lived through a war," Lt. Newcomb explained. "We saw death all around us. Lots of people were killed just for being a problem, for being in the way. For us, that's not a strange question. It's a real worry."

"Don't worry," Rabbi Cohen replied calmly. "Don't worry. For us, every life is sacred. We do not kill at all, ever! Yes, you are a problem, but we will solve the problem in a way that is good for you. If we didn't care about our fellow humans, we wouldn't be planning to save all the others in Nowhere. We would just leave them there. They're not causing us any problems where they are. However, we can't leave them. They are human beings, and their lives are important to us. We have to save them and find an answer that is good for them."

"Okay," Jen said, taking charge of the discussion. "Let's review. We can't take the lost people back to their own times. We can't take them into the past, and we can't bring them into the future. Ideas."

"Maybe we're coming at the problem from the wrong direction," Mike suggested. "We know what we can't do. How about making a list of what we need. Correction. What these people need. Maybe that will lead us to an answer."

"They're human beings," Allie said. "To find happiness, they need what all humans beings need."

"Humans need to live their lives," Nick began. "They need to live, grow old, and die."

"Humans need food and shelter," Allie said.

"Humans need families," Mike added. "All of us need to find someone to live our lives with. We need to have children. We need to create families that live on after us."

"Humans need to build," Jen said. "Humans need to create civilizations. They need space."

"Humans need to explore and to learn," Mike added. "We're time teams. We're proof of that."

"That's a big order to fill," Jen said. "It's like we're describing this world. The problem is we can't find a place for them on this world."

Allie's eyes widened. Everyone knew she had just had a brilliant idea. "If we can't find a place for them on this world, maybe we find them another world. In fact, we have already found another world. Kwasi's there right now."

"Minor problem," Nick said. "That world belongs to someone else."

"Right," Allie argued. "Those beings live in eleven dimensions. The people we're talking about live in four dimensions. The other beings wouldn't be aware of the humans, and the humans wouldn't be aware of them. They can all live on the same world in different dimensions. It's perfect."

"Perfect if they'll go along with it," Nick warned. "We have to ask permission."

"Okay,' Jen said. "We'll ask. Just in case they agree, we need to do some more planning. We can't just drop off a bunch of people and say, 'Have a nice life."

"Nowhere is full of things they can use," Allie added. "We can get tools, food, and equipment from all the ships and planes. Sails will make good tents and clothing. They'll have wood and metal. They'll have medical supplies."

"Kwasi's ship was carrying cows, sheep, pigs, and chickens," Mike said with excitement. He could see the solution to the problem taking shape right before his eyes. "Elizabeth's father's ship was carrying cows too. The dog sled has a team of dogs, so humans won't be without their best friend. This brave new world will get off to real a good start."

"Think of the skills all these people have," Nick said. "There are mechanics, carpenters, doctors, farmers, sailors, fishermen, you name it. There's even a real good hunter."

"They'll be far better off than early humans were," Allie said, "and they managed to spread all over the earth without any of those tools or skills. They'll be better off than the colonists coming to the New World. They didn't have all the advantages these people will have. This new human colony should do very well."

"Most of the people in Nowhere are men," Jen said. "That's going to make it hard to start families."

"There are a lot of women," Mike noted. "Kwasi has twenty of them with him. A lot of those sailors brought their wives with them. There may be more men at first, but that will even out in a generation. The first babies will be born within a year. Half of them will be boys and half will be girls."

"Final problem," Jen announced. "We're going to have to rescue all those people. That's not going to be easy. Ideas."

"We're gonna need rope," Mike said. "We should have lots of it. Every search team will have to be tied together when it goes into Nowhere. We'll have to drag equipment and supplies we salvage from the ships and planes into the new world."

How are we going to get ahold of people who are above and below us?" Allie asked. "Nick can't reach everybody by climbing on Kwasi's shoulders."

"I was thinking about an extension ladder," Nick said. "They're made of aluminum, so they're light and easy to carry."

"Rope and extension ladders," Jen said. "Anything else?"

"I wish we had more than one dog," Mike said. "Menlo will have to lead all those search teams and he's gonna get pretty tired." Mike stopped talking and looked stunned, like he had just remembered something horrible. "Menlo," he said. "We left him with Kwasi. When we go back, how are we going to find the new world? We can go in through the opening in the Triangle. How are we going to find the other opening? Only Menlo could do that."

"I've been thinking about an idea," Nick answered. "I need to go to the lab tomorrow. I wish Lenore was here to help me. I could use a hand." Nick remembered Bashir. "He still works there doesn't he?" he asked the adults. Dr. Newcomb and Rabbi Cohen both nodded. "Fine. He'll do just fine," Nick said with confidence.

"That about wraps it up," Jen said. "We'll stay at the Institute one more day. Nick, you'll be at the lab. The rest of us will gather lots of rope and an extension ladder. We'll get back to Nowhere by following Lt. Newcomb's Avenger. We know the door is open at that moment."

Mike turned to Lt. Newcomb. "That explains your third radar blip," he said. "It was us – twice." Lt. Newcomb nodded. His eyes were still red from crying.

"We've developed a good plan," Jen announced as she stood. "Thanks guys."

"Just a moment of your time before you go," Rabbi Cohen said to the time crew. "Dr. Newcomb and I have been amazed. We just learned how you come up with solutions. You talk to each other. You all throw out ideas and build a plan. It was fascinating to watch."

"That's the way Patrick gets ideas from Mike and Nick," Jen said. "When my crew began to work with his team, he taught us. That's his leadership method. He says 'Ideas' and invites everyone to think out loud. No idea is foolish or stupid. They all get listened to. He gets everyone's brain working on the problem. It's a lot better than just one guy making all the decisions."

"Very interesting," Dr. Newcomb said. "Perhaps this is another skill all cadets should learn. Rabbi Cohen and I will talk to the other teachers about this. Thank you for sharing it with us."

The group said goodbye to Lt. Newcomb and Ensign Dubois. "We'll take you with us," Jen told the two flyers. "We'll come by to get you the day after tomorrow."

"You made it sound exciting to be part of this new colony," Ensign Dubois said. "I still would rather go back to my parents. I know I can't, so I'm looking forward to a new adventure and a new life in the new world. How about you Chuck?" he asked his friend. Lt. Newcomb nodded as tears rolled down his cheek.

CHAPTER FIFTEEN
THE NOWHERE POSITIONING
SYSTEM

"What are you guys gonna do the rest of the afternoon?" Jen asked the others as they left the UNH Medical Center.

"I'm heading to the lab to find Bashir," Nick answered. "I'm hoping to get in a couple of hours of work before the end of the day. It'll make tomorrow easier if we get a head start."

"Allie and I are S/Os," Mike said. "I think we should do what S/Os are best at. We need to research the history of colonies. We're hoping to start a new human colony on a new world. We want to do this thing right and avoid as many mistakes as possible." Allie nodded in agreement. She and Mike would spend the afternoon studying.

"Patrick taught me something else," Jen added with a smile. "While the engineers are in the lab and the S/Os are studying, the pool is the best place for a pilot. I'm going to enjoy a couple of quite hours in the sun. I'll make dinner, and it'll be ready at six. Be on time, or go hungry."

▲

The next morning Nick was up and out early. "We learned a lot yesterday," Allie told Jen. "Humanity has a real bad history. We have a lot of things to warn Lt. Newcomb and Ensign Dubois about. We're going to visit them at the medical center. When we get back from there, we'll prepare for tomorrow's mission."

Allie and Mike found Lt. Newcomb and Ensign Dubois on the porch. They pulled up chairs and got comfortable, as they planned on being there a while. "Gentlemen," Mike began, "We have been studying the history of colonies. We want this one to start out with every possible advantage. Knowing what happened in the past may help you avoid the same mistakes." Mike set up a hologram projector. The two flyers had been through similar presentations during the war, when they were briefed on bombing missions. They paid close attention. They realized their survival could depend on this information.

Allie began. "From the earliest times humans have been creating colonies," she said. The holograph showed a map of the world. "Humanity began in Africa. All humans are curious. It's one of the things that make us human. From the beginning, they needed to explore. A group of people would leave the bigger group and go live on the other side of the hill." Little red dots showed the human colonies as people moved around Africa. "They did this over and over so that eventually, Africa had lots of little colonies. In time, humans moved north out of Africa. Some went east into Asia. Others went west into Europe.

"These colonies were different from the one you're going to live in," Allie continued. "If people didn't like the new side of the hill, they could always return. You won't be able to go back. You'll be in the same situation as the humans who went to Australia and to North America. They were stuck there, and were on their own." Red dots on the holographic screen showed people moving into these two new continents.

"The best documented colonies were the English, French, and Spanish colonies in America and English colonies in Australia and New Zealand. Some colonies did fine, while other colonies failed. Gentlemen, you can't fail, because you can't call for help. No one will be coming back to rescue you."

"Colonies that succeeded focused on their children and invested their efforts in making the future better for the next generation," Mike said. "They loved their children and they educated them. Gentlemen, you must start schools right away and teach your children everything you know. Have everyone in the colony write down what they know and start a library for your children and for you children's children."

"Avoid humanity's worst problem," Allie said. "It will be hard because it's part of our nature. Some people always try to control the others. People will kill to get control. They will fight wars. They will starve people. They will do the most horrible things, just to get power and control."

"We know," Ensign Dubois said. "The Lieutenant and I have just lived through the biggest war people have ever fought. The war started because some countries wanted to   control others."

Mike banged his open hand on his forehead. The gesture said he had just remembered something important. "Allie, you just said leaders in the past starved people to control them. This world - our world - became peaceful when leaders couldn't do that anymore."

Allie made the same gesture as Mike. "Yes," she said with excitement. "How could we have forgotten? We need to bring lots of Dr. MacDonald's grain with us. If the colony plants that, no one can ever control food. People can grow their own everywhere."

"It solves another problem," Mike added. "They can make clean bio-fuels. They don't have to pollute the new world to get energy. How could we have forgotten the most important thing in history? Gentlemen, I am even surer now that this new colony will be okay."

Mike paused. He wasn't sure how to express his next thought. It could be a sensitive matter. He wanted to tell them about Kwasi. The two flyers came from 1945, a time of racism in America. In some places in 1945 African Americans weren't even allowed to sit at a lunch counter or on a bus with white Americans. Mike began by saying, "In the new world you will meet an amazing guy who has become my friend. His name is Kwasi. He was a slave in Jamaica. Kwasi is smart and he is a natural leader. You two must work with him."

"I grew up in Baltimore," Lt. Newcomb said. "I know lots of African Americans and I'm not prejudiced. Besides, my son Junior is going to be a civil rights lawyer. I can't be with him as he grows, but in the new world I will do the same kind of work he will do. I'll work hard to make sure everyone has equal rights, and that everyone gets along. I would want my son to be proud of his Dad."

"The Lieutenant and I are airmen," Ensign Dubois added. "We do a hard and dangerous job and we respect other people who do the same job - fly in combat. I heard about the Tuskegee Airmen. They are black fighter pilots. They not only had to fight the enemy, they had to fight our own army just to become flyers. I respect them. I respect Kwasi and I will work with him."

"If you don't let racism get a foothold in the new world, it will never happen," Mike said. "Kids aren't born racist. They learn racism from their parents. A lot of the women in the new colony are African. In a couple of generations there will be no black people and no white people. Everyone will be brown."

"We've got a lot to do before tomorrow," Allie said as she stood. "We'll come by to get you in the morning. Gentlemen, the rest of your lives will be an incredible adventure. You are about to become leaders in a settlement of humans on a new world. This is an amazing time."

Nick returned from the lab in the afternoon. "I need you guys to come to the arrival/departure pad," he told Jen, Allie, and Mike. "I found a way to find time craft without Menlo."

They arrived to find two craft waiting on the pad. One was the Auckland. A group of eight maintenance workers was also there, waiting for Nick. "You know how the Global

Positioning System works," Nick said to his friends. "Your car's GPS gets signals from a bunch of satellites in space and uses these signals to calculate its position. It's gonna be a bit harder for us because we'll only have two signals, and they are always changing places." Everyone looked a bit confused but kept listening.

"Couldn't we just use the Time Craft Locator?" Mike asked. "It worked before when we had to find the Auckland."

"No," Nick answered. "The TCL measures distance to a craft, and there are no dimensions in Nowhere. Still, the TCL and my new idea have something in common. They both pick up brain waves from the craft's mental interface switches. I know that nothing mechanical or electronic works in Nowhere. That's why this device uses brain waves to track brain waves.

"Ladies and gentlemen," Nick said, turning to the maintenance workers. "Let's begin." The eight workers each stood at a corner of one of the two craft and lifted. They began to walk around carrying the craft. They walked towards each other, and then they walked away in different directions. They were not walking in any pattern. They just walked where they felt like going, all the time carrying a craft. "Good," Nick called to them. "Good. Keep it up."

Jen, Allie, and Mike were still confused. "This is as close as I could get to what happens in Nowhere," Nick explained. "Everything keeps shifting and scrambling. That's why I can't measure distance. There isn't any. Menlo finds things because he doesn't use his eyes. He uses his nose. It doesn't matter to him if something isn't where it was a minute ago. He follows its smell.

"That's what this does," he said holding up a new gadget. "It receives brain wave signals from each of the time craft. It uses the two signals to figure out how you have to walk to get to one of them. Since the craft are always moving this thing is always calculating. It has this arrow here that you follow."

Everyone crowded around Nick to see the arrow. "Nick," Mike yelled. "That's my GPS. You took my GPS! That was my birthday present. I told you before. Leave my stuff alone."

"Shush," Allie said to Mike, putting her finger to her lips.

"Allie, he took my present," Mike complained. "Don't you care?"

"Mike, shush," Allie said firmly. "This is important."

Mike threw his arms in the air and rolled his eyes. He turned around to see if anyone would agree with him, but there was no one behind him. They were all gathered around Nick.

Nick turned on the GPS and the arrow appeared on the screen. "I've set it for the Auckland," he said while the workers continued to wander anywhere they felt like going. The arrow on the screen kept pointing at the Auckland no matter where it went. Nick covered his eyes so he couldn't watch the time craft. He could only look down at the GPS screen in his hand. Without seeing the craft he was able to follow the Auckland wherever the workers carried it.

"I'll switch to the other craft," he said. Now, he began to follow it. "It works the other way too," he told his friends. He signaled the workers to set down the craft. "Cover your eyes Jen," he said, handing the pilot the GPS. "Don't look at the craft just wander where you feel like going. The needle will keep pointing toward the craft."

Jen looked like she was lost as she wandered aimlessly around the arrival/departure pad. "It works," she called. "The arrow keeps changing." Just to be sure, Nick had the workers move the Auckland without Jen seeing. She kept following the needle right to her craft.

"It works in the test," Nick warned. "I guess it will work in Nowhere, but we'll find out when we get there."

The next morning Mike and Allie went to the Medical Center to get Lt. Newcomb and Ensign Dubois, and brought them to the arrival/departure pad. Meanwhile, Jen and Nick had loaded the craft. It was cramped inside. The two airmen and Nick were too tall for the seating platforms, so they sat on the floor. Mike and Allie sat on one side of the craft, while Jen stood at the pilot's position. The other seating platform was piled high with boxes of Dr. MacDonald's seeds. The extension ladder barely fit. Nick had to put it in catty corner. This meant everyone had to lean to one side to avoid hitting the ladder with their heads. The rest of the space in the craft was taken up with rope and other supplies.

"Nick, what's in that box?" Mike asked, pointing at a flat carton on top of the seeds.

"Duct tape," Nick answered. "Never leave home without it. It's an engineer's best friend."

Jen programmed in the sequence and frame for the moment when the Avenger entered Nowhere, and flew the Auckland close on the bomber's tail. "Just think," Mike said. "We're out there too, on our first trip into Nowhere. If the CT 9225 wasn't cloaked maybe I could see myself seeing myself looking out the window. You know what they say about time travel messing with your mind."

Jen followed the Avenger until its propeller stopped. "We should wait until all of us are lost," Jen said. "We don't want to create any problems by being in two places at once." The four time travelers and the two airmen watched the other Lt. Dubois get out of the Avenger. The other Lt. Newcomb followed him. They looked scared. Ensign Dubois grabbed Lt. Newcomb's parachute strap and then, they disappeared.

Next, the two time craft uncloaked. The people in the Auckland II watched Patrick and the other Jen get out. The pilots spoke to each other and disappeared. Charmaine and the other Nick and Lenore got out next. Nick spoke to Lenore and all three disappeared. The other Mike and the other Allie got out. Mike had Menlo on a leash. He smiled at Allie and she blew him a kiss. She disappeared. Mike bent over to straighten Menlo's collar, he stood up, and they both disappeared.

"All clear," Jen announced. "Let's go. Mike, tie us together. We'll leave the Auckland here so it marks the doorway for us. We can use the GPS to find it later. We can bring the seed to the colony then. Lt. Newcomb and Ensign Dubois, do you mind carrying the rope and the ladder? You're bigger and stronger than we are."

Jen held the GPS in front of her. "Wait," Nick said. "I forgot. We need two signals to find our way. We can probably find the CT 9225 in Nowhere, but then how do we find the other world? We would need the CT 9225 to be in the new world's doorway. To top it off, we don't have Menlo. I didn't think this one through."

"The arrow is pointing to my left," Jen said. "I'm getting some sort of signal. Ideas crew?"

"It must be the CT 9225," Nick said. "It's the only other time craft in here."

"We might as well find it," Allie added. "Once we have it we're one step closer to our plan." Jen looked at Mike, asking for his opinion. He nodded.

"We're on the hunt," Jen said as she led the line of people into Nowhere. "I guess this isn't a GPS anymore, Nick. It's a Nowhere Positioning System. It's an NPS."

CHAPTER SIXTEEN
LOVE HURTS

Nick's Nowhere Positioning System worked. Jen followed the arrow as it moved, always pointing towards the CT 9225. Once, the arrow pointed backwards. The group had to make a wide turn to go the way it pointed. They walked a lot, but at last Jen announced, "I see the other doorway into the new world."

"How can that be?" Nick asked. "The NPS should have taken us to the CT 9225."

"There's the answer," Jen replied. The parade of four time travelers and two Navy flyers realized why they had arrived at the doorway. The CT 9225 was already there, just inside.

The time travelers were surprised by what they saw as they passed through the opening. The new world had changed since they had left. The flyers were surprised too. They had never been to the new world, but this was not what the time travelers had described to them.

Kwasi was sitting on the grass. Charmaine was sitting beside him and he had his arm around her shoulder. She leaned her head on his shoulder and Menlo sat beside them. All of them had their backs to the doorway and did not see their friends arrive from Nowhere. Kwasi, Charmaine, and Menlo were looking over two rows of neat and carefully built, round huts with cone-shaped, grass roofs. The small village, with one long street, had been built near the stream. Smoke was rising from cooking fires inside some of the huts. There were far more people here now than when the time travelers had left. Some people were working in the street outside the huts, while others were sitting in doorways relaxing.

"Look," Mike said. "There's Patrick." He pointed at a figure walking in their direction up the street between the huts. Menlo heard Mike's voice. He jumped up and ran to his master. Mike got down on his knee and hugged his dog. He kissed Menlo on the muzzle while Menlo lapped his face. The dog's tail was wagging so fast and hard it looked like it might break off.

Kwasi and Charmaine turned to see what had excited Menlo. They too stood up and ran to their friends. Everyone hugged and shook hands. Menlo was so excited he couldn't control himself. He put his tail down and ran in circles around the group of hugging people. As he ran he bayed in joy. *Arrroo-roo-roo. Arrroo-roo-roo. Arrroo-roo-roo.*

Menlo's barking told everyone else in the small village that something important was happening. People came out of the huts and started to run toward the small crowd with a dog running in circles around it. Patrick was one of the first to arrive and he joined in the greeting. Menlo kept running in circles and baying.

"Lenore's here too," Patrick told the others. Lenore arrived and the hugging started all over again. Menlo kept running. The women from Africa arrived. They knew the time crews, and they all hugged while Menlo kept running. Sally and Elizabeth arrived. Jen and Allie picked up the small girls and hugged them. They passed the girls to others for more hugs. Menlo kept running.

The new people arrived. "Everybody," Kwasi called loudly, holding his arms up so they would listen to him. Menlo finally stopped running and came to Mike for another hug. "Deese are deh people Ah tol' you about. Deese are Patrick's and Lenore's friens. Dey hab come back!" The crowd smiled and nodded. Some mumbled hello. One of the people was an Arab woman; another was the Inuit mother, holding her baby. They had only learned a few words of English, so other villagers used hand gestures to explain that these were Kwasi's friends.

"Come, Mahk," Kwasi said, putting his arm around Mike's shoulder. "Come and tell me what you hab done."

The hunter sat again on the grass. The villagers wandered back to what they had been doing before the newcomers arrived, while the new arrivals sat with Kwasi in a big circle. Meanwhile, Menlo went from person to person giving kisses and getting hugs and pats.

"First, you need to tell us what you have done, Kwasi," Mike said pointing toward the village. "How did you do this so fast?"

"Mahk, you hab been gone two months," Kwasi said. He was surprised that his friend didn't seem to know how long he had been away.

"Two months?" Mike asked. He looked at Jen, Allie, and Nick. They all shrugged their shoulders. They had only been back at the Time Institute for two days. Time travel messes with you mind, but so does inter-dimensional travel.

"Something happened we don't understand," Allie added. "Kwasi, we were only gone two days. For you, we were gone two months. I don't know why. Anyway, tell us what happened. Everything is changed."

"Ah am getting used to lots of strange tings and tings dat change," Kwasi said. "Aftah you left, Ah fed dah women and dah babies. Deh dog and Ah, we caught fish. I made a bow and arrows, and a spear. We hunted meat, deh dog and Ah. Deh animals here are strange, but dey taste good. Deh plants are different dan in Africa, but deh women, dey know what make a plant good to eat. Dey get dah good plants for us.

"It is cold at nahght here. It began to rain. Ah knew we needed to make huts to keep us warm and dry. Deh women, dey worked wid me. We made deh huts lahke in Africa. Dey are in nice rows. Dah rows let people visit and talk to each udder. Dat's good for people, to see der neighbors. It's good for deh children. Deh adults watch deh kids for deh neighbors.

"Once we got a billage built and deh people fed, deh dog and Ah, we went out dah door to dat strange place you call Nowhere, where deh people are all lost. When Ah see someone, Ah tie deh rope to dem. I bring dem back here. Dey are really afraid at first. Ah'm getting' used to dis place and all deh strange stuff. But, when Ah touch someone dat's lost and dey can see udder people, dey are afraid at first.

"Deh women, dey teach deh new people what dey need to know to lib here. Ah teach dem too. Ah hab dem help me make tings. We hab made a billage, just like in Africa."

How about you, Patrick?" Mike asked his friend. "How long have you been here?"

"Only a couple of days," Patrick answered. "I'm a newcomer. Lenore's been here longer, a little more than a week."

"The CT 9225 was already here when Kwasi brought me in," Lenore said. She shrugged her shoulders to show that she did not know how the craft got to this place.

"Ah found it and Ah knew it must be your udder ship," Kwasi added. "Ah figured it was safe here."

"Good thing you did," Jen said. "We may not have gotten back here without it." She held up Nick's NPS. "This is a great tool, but it only works if there are two time craft. We needed the CT 9225 to be here in order to find our way."

"We've been rude," Mike said suddenly. "Kwasi, these two men are Lt. Newcomb and Ensign Dubois. They are the men who brought us here, the men who escaped through the doorway. Jen, Lenore, and Allie found them. They fought in a war that happened long after your time. People had flying machines, and these two men flew one of those machines."

Kwasi's eyes opened wide. He had imagined how wonderful it would be to fly like a bird. Was it possible these men had actually done that? "Lt. Newcomb and Ensign Dubois know everything that has happened," Mike continued. "They understand the plan we have figured out, and why it has to be that way. Kwasi, do you like this place enough to stay here the rest of your life? Would you be willing to help all the people here, and all the people in Nowhere build a new world?"

"Most of all, Mahk, Ah wanna go back to my family in Africa," Kwasi answered. "Long ago Ah knew dat would neber happen. In mah heart, Ah hab said goodbye to dem. Ah don' wanna go back an' be a slabe again. Dat was awful. Dis is a good place. Ah could be happy here. Ah can hunt.

Ah can visit wid mah neighbors. Ah can play wid dah children. Yeah, Ah could stay here."

Allie and Jen noticed something the others did not. It was Charmaine, and she looked distressed. They moved over to her and formed a huddle, beginning their own conversation.

"We need to get permission for you to stay here," Mike continued. "Have you seen that strange man without a face?"

"Yeah," Kwasi said. "He come to see me twice. Dis world has tree moons. When deh moons are all in deh sky deh same nahght, he come deh next day. He told me deh moons all pull together and he can use dis pull."

"He's using gravity to project himself into four dimensions," Mike said to the others.

"Yeah," Dat's deh word he used," Kwasi said. "Grabidy."

"When's the next time this happens?" Mike asked Kwasi.

"Der were two moons last nahght. Der will be tree tonahght. Tomorrow he can come."

"What else did he say?" Allie asked.

"He asked me a lot about me and what mah lahfe is lahke. He wanna know how I see mah world. I tell him Ah see, Ah hear, Ah touch, Ah taste, Ah smell. He wanna know how Ah hear, what sound is lahke. He asked about touchin' tings, how dey feel, what feelin' is lahke. He wanna know how food taste, how tings smell, what smellin' and tastin' is lahke. It's hard to tell someone deese tings. I don't know how dey are. Dey just are.

"Ah ask him about himself. He try to tell me tings, but he is bery strange. Ah understand his words," Kwasi explained. "Ah don' always understand what dey mean. He don' speak clear."

"He's curious about us," Mike said. "He wants to know what living in four dimensions is like. It sounds like he tried to describe living in eleven dimensions. We can't understand that, so his words won't make sense.

"I'm hoping compassion and guilt are things he experiences. When he learns the harm he's done to all these people, maybe he will want to help them. That's the big unknown in our plan. If he says yes, we're in business. If he says no, we're back to the drawing board.

"We need to be ready," Mike continued. "Patrick, Lenore. We need to fill you in on all we've learned about Nowhere and about this place. We need to fill you in on the plan we developed. To be honest, I don't like being the guy who makes the decisions. Patrick, I want you and Jen to take over the responsibility. You're trained for that."

The group broke up. Kwasi invited Lt. Newcomb and Ensign Dubois to tour the village. Mike and Nick stayed with Patrick and Lenore to get them up to speed with all that had happened.

Jen and Allie left the others and walked off with Charmaine. Menlo knew Mike's meeting would be boring, so he went with the girls. "Okay," Jen said to Charmaine. "Fill us in?"

"On what?" Charmaine asked, pretending she didn't understand the question.

"On you and Kwasi," Allie answered. "What's going on? Don't try to tell us you're just friends."

"We're far beyond friends," Charmaine confessed. "I love him. He's the most wonderful man I've ever met. He's so kind and gentle. Then, he's so strong and sure. He's so wise, but sometimes he's so innocent. He's so smart. He learns everything right away. He already knows all sorts of things about this place. He knows the animals. He knows the plants. He's explored. He knows his way around.

"Look what he built in such a short time. Meanwhile, he took care of everyone and even rescued more people. I know he has a strong accent and his English isn't good. That doesn't mean he's not smart."

"Of course not," Allie added. "Dr. Newcomb taught us that in his Ethics class. There is no difference between us and anyone in the past. We used to call these people primitive. What an insult that was. People have always been just as smart as we are. They just didn't have our technology. We only have that technology because we built on the knowledge they gave us."

"What about Kwasi?" Jen asked. "Does he feel the same about you?"

"Oh yes. He says he loves me just like I love him. He makes up poetry for me. At night around the fires he recites his poems about me. It's in his language, so I don't understand, but the women do. They all sigh and get the love light in their eyes. I know the poems must be beautiful. I can see the love in Kwasi's eyes when he is reciting them to me."

"I understand," Allie said. "That's every girl's dream, a handsome guy reciting love poetry to her in a foreign language." She sighed at the thought.

"You looked hurt when Mike asked Kwasi if he would want to stay here," Jen said.

"Yes," Charmaine answered with tears in her eyes. "I know Kwasi can't go back to his own time, and he can't come to mine. I was in Room 307 when we all talked about this. I knew we weren't meant to ever know each other, never mind fall in love and live our lives together. I knew this moment would come, eventually. I just tried not to think about it. I hoped keeping it out of my mind would keep it from happening."

"Does Lenore know?" Allie asked.

"Yes. When I'm not with Kwasi all I do is talk to Lenore about him."

Jen stopped walking and hugged Charmaine. "Girl, no one else understands this like I do. In Alexandria, I fell in love with a beautiful man named Philip." Menlo saw Jen hugging Charmaine and jumped up to join in. He kissed each on the face. "It was a love that wasn't meant to be," Jen continued, wiping her freshly kissed face. "I'm sorry to tell you this, but you're in for a world of hurt. It will hurt more than you can imagine. That's the bad news. The good news is you do get over it. I found Patrick, right under my nose. If I had the chance now I wouldn't swap him for Philip. There's another guy for you, Charmaine. When you get over the hurt, that other guy will walk into your life and you'll be happy again."

Jen and Allie walked on each side of Charmaine. Each had an arm around her shoulder while Charmaine sobbed. Menlo lapped her hand, trying to make her feel better.

CHAPTER SEVENTEEN
WELCOME TO YOUR NEW HOME

The next day Kwasi, the two flyers, and the time travelers gathered at the spot where the eleven-dimensional being had appeared previously. He was on time. "A greater mind," he said as he appeared. He still looked like a mannequin in a store window. He had a body and a head, but no features. "Why is your mind bigger than before?'

Mike nudged Patrick to step forward and answer. "No way," Patrick said to his S/O. "I'm in charge, and I just made you spokesperson. You do the talking." He pushed Mike ahead of the group.

Mike stepped toward the being and said, "There are more of us here now. Perhaps you do not experience us as individuals. Perhaps you feel more of us thinking."

"Individuals?" the being asked. "What does that mean?"

"We are not one," Mike answered. "We are divided so that each of us lives in a body. Each has a mind. We have to communicate with sound. We have to tell each other our thoughts. "

"You are not one?" the being asked. "You are separated into many? That is why you have these things called names." He seemed happy to have learned something new about four-dimensional beings. "How do you communicate?"

"We speak," Mike said. "I am speaking to you now. We communicate by making sounds with an opening called a mouth. The others know what I am saying to you because they hear me. They hear my sound through openings called ears."

"We are many, but all one," the being said. Mike knew he could never understand the being's statement because he lived in only four dimensions. "Each of us thinks, but we all know the thoughts," the being continued. "We do not need to communicate. We all know. I built the machine to search for you. The others knew what I was doing. They know what we are saying now. They learn as I learn from you.

"You seem different this time," the being said to Mike. "Are you another?"

"My name is Mike. We spoke the first time. The next two times you spoke with another named Kwasi. He is here, and he is hearing our words."

"I have so much to ask you," the being said to Mike.

"Yes," Mike replied. "First, I have learned many things since you spoke to me. I understand your machine better. You need to know we did not come here searching for the source of your signal. Your machine caused us to be trapped here. It has hurt us.

"What is hurt?" the being asked.

"It is harm." Mike answered.

"I don't understand harm."

"Great," Mike thought to himself. "In eleven dimensions nothing ever goes wrong, so he can't understand hurt or harm. Wrong. Maybe that's the word I need.

"Hurt is when things are wrong for us," Mike explained. "Your machine has made things wrong for us. It takes us from our four dimensions and traps us in a place with no dimensions. It takes us out of time that moves into the future and leaves us in a place with no time. It takes us from a place where there are others like us and leaves us alone. It takes us from a place where we do things and leaves us where we do nothing. It takes us from a place where we age and die and puts us where we never age. That place is all wrong for us."

The being was silent. Mike wondered what he was doing. He hoped he was transmitting his thoughts to the rest of the eleven-dimensional beings. Mike continued, "Imagine if you were taken from the others and trapped in only four dimensions."

That worked. "That would be wrong for us," the being replied. "We are meant to be together and to share our thoughts. We cannot imagine being apart. Thinking about it makes us feel strange. We do not like this strange feeling. We want it to stop. Is that hurt?"

"Yes," Mike answered. He was pleased to have taught the being a new idea. The being was silent again. Mike guessed he and the others were pondering this new idea of hurt.

"I did not want to hurt you," the being answered. "My calculations said four-dimensional beings should exist. I wanted to prove myself right. I did not mean to make things wrong for you. Can you go back to where things are right? Can my machine help you to go back?"

"No," Mike answered. "What is done is done. We can never go back to our world. However, you can help us move from the place that is wrong to one that is right."

There was silence. "We agree we should help you to go to a place that is right for you. Will that stop the hurt?"

"We will never see the others we knew on our world," Mike said. "That is hurt. However, everyone who is in the wrong place will be together in the new right place. They can live their lives again. That is the best you can do for them."

Silence. "We want to do this best for them," the being said. "Tell me how. We must hurry. The moons are moving apart."

"This is the answer," Mike said speaking more quickly. "Many of us are now on your world. You are in eleven dimensions. Without your machine you don't know we are here. We are in four dimensions, and don't know you are here. We do not affect each other in any way. We can both live on this world without knowing about each other.

"We ask you to let us move here to live. Let us live out our lives. Let us grow in number and build what we need, to be in a place that is right for us."

There was more silence. It went on so long Mike began to wonder if the moons had moved too far apart and the being was unable to stay in contact. However, the figure did not disappear. It stood there without moving, just like a mannequin. Finally, the being spoke. "We agree," he said. "We ask one thing. This was our world first. We want you to respect our world and do nothing to harm it."

"We agree," Mike answered. "We thank you. Next, we have to find all the beings like us who are trapped where things are wrong. We must bring them here to where things are right. We have to prepare and have work to do. Please do not turn off your machine. Wait until the moons are together the next time. Come again to ask us if we are ready. Turn of the machine then."

"Agreed," the being said. "Welcome to our world. May things always be right for you here. I cannot stay any longer. I will come back when the moons are together again. I will make sure everything is right before I turn off the machine."

The being disappeared. Mike turned to his friends and they rushed at him. Allie threw her arms around his neck. "You were wonderful," she said. "I'm so proud of you."

"Great job, Brains," Patrick added, patting him on the back. Nick shook his hand. Jen, Lenore, and Charmaine took turns hugging him.

"Kwasi, Lt. Newcomb, Ensign Dubois," Mike said. "Welcome to your new home. Remember what the being said. Take good care of it. It's the only world you've got."

As it grew dark, Patrick, Nick, and Mike went to Kwasi's hut with him. Jen, Lenore, Allie, and Charmaine went to another hut with some of the African women. In Kwasi's hut Mike found a stringed musical instrument with a neck like a guitar. The body was made from a hollow gourd and had an animal skin stretched over it. "What's this, Kwasi?" Mike asked.

"Dat is a donso ngoni," Kwasi answered. "In mah language dat means a 'hunter's harp.' Ah'm a hunter, but Ah don' play deh harp bery well. Ah built it to make me feel good. I make some simple music. It reminds me of Africa. Deh women lahk it too. Dey tink of home."

"It reminds me of a banjo," Mike said as he began to pluck the strings. "Yes, it's definitely an early type of banjo. I think I could play this if I practice a bit." He began to pick out a tune.

"Ah made some drums too," Kwasi said proudly as he showed off his work. His drums were made from tree trunks he had hollowed out. He had stretched animal skins over the hollow bodies. "A don' play deese well. But dey make a sound dat remind me of home." He played the drums with his open hands.

"Can I try?" Patrick asked. "I play drums, but I play with drumsticks," he added, picking up some shafts Kwasi was making into arrows. "Let me give you a beat, Mike." The two started to jam together.

"Can you make a ngoni that is longer?" Nick asked. "I need only four heavy strings and a bigger gourd."

"Yeah," Kwasi said agreeably. "Ah will make one for you tomorrow. You work wid me and Ah make it for you just dah way you wan' it."

"Could you make a couple of other drums? I need a small, flat one and a bigger, deeper one," Patrick asked.

"Sure," Kwasi said, smiling. He was happy his friends were interested in learning to play his instruments. "You work wid me and Nick tomorrow."

"We've got a month before the next time the moons are all together," Mike said. "I'm betting the Sirens will get pretty good on these instruments by then. We'll make evenings around here a lot of fun. We'll play the first concerts in this new world."

The next morning the time travelers, the two flyers, and Kwasi assembled again on the grassy area looking over the village. "Jen and I made up a list of things we need to accomplish before the machine is turned off," Patrick told the group. "I want to get your ideas. First, we've got to save the people in Nowhere. How are we going to do that?"

"It would be better to go out as small teams, rather than sending one large search party," Allie said.

"There's only one Menlo," Nick added. "We can't risk going out into Nowhere without him. We could lose our search teams and end up worse off than we are now."

"The Inuit dog sled has a bunch of huskies still in harness," Mike said. "I saw the dogs when I found the baby. If we find the sled we can bring the dogs back here and Kwasi can train them. Then, each team would have its own dog. That will make finding the people out there a lot easier, and a lot faster."

"Ah will ask deh baby's mudder for sometin' of hers," Kwasi said. "Ah will have deh dog smell it. Den, he will find deh sled. Dat dog has a good nose."

"These are all good ideas," Jen said. She became very serious. "It really worries me that we will not find every one of the wanderers. If anyone is still in Nowhere when the being turns off the machine...." She didn't complete her sentence. Everyone nodded and looked at the ground. They all knew what Jen meant. Anyone left in Nowhere would wander forever. There would be no hope. "We can't do that to a fellow human," Jen added. "We can't miss anyone. We have to make sure we get them all."

"Most of the people who got trapped in Nowhere went in with someone else," Allie said. "We need to ask everyone here and everyone we find, to make a list of who was on their ship or plane. We can check people off the list as we bring them here. That way, we'll know who we're missing and how many. We just have to hope no one was alone when they got trapped in Nowhere."

"Good idea," Patrick said. Mike smiled proudly at Allie. "We need someone in charge of the lists," Patrick added. "Charmaine, will you take on that job?" Charmaine nodded.

"Lt. Newcomb and Ensign Dubois," Jen said to the two flyers. "Each person we rescue is going to need help adjusting to this place. You saw the people wandering alone. They don't know they're lost. They're stuck in Now doing what they were doing when they got trapped.

"When we save them they'll be scared and confused. They need to understand what happened to them. They need to know they are staying here for the rest of their lives. They will all want to go home and will need help to accepting that they can't go back, that they must stay here. You two have already gone through this. You're the best people to help the others." The two flyers nodded. They would do this job.

"Once we get all the people out of Nowhere, we need to start salvaging the equipment on the planes and ships," Nick said. "Lenore and I are engineers. I think we should be in charge of that. We know how to take things apart." Jen and Patrick agreed. This was a job for the engineers.

"Make it so, Mr. LaForge," Patrick said.

"Huh?" Nick asked.

"Never mind," Patrick said, annoyed that Nick had missed the joke. "You got the job."

"While the engineers are taking things apart the search teams should round up all the animals lost in Nowhere," Mike said. "Sally told me there were cows on her father's ship."

"Der were cows and pigs and chickens on mah boat," Kwasi said. "Dey will gib us milk and eggs. I will hunt deh meat for ebryone."

"You guys are great," Patrick said to the group. "We've developed a good plan. Tomorrow we go out to find the dog sled and the huskies. Kwasi, you can start training them right away. We'll have search teams working in a couple of days."

"We've forgotten and important detail," Allie said. Everyone turned to look at her. "When we arrived the second time with Lt. Newcomb and Ensign Dubois, we watched ourselves get lost in Nowhere. Are our doubles still there, and what do we do if we find them?"

"Time travel does mess with your mind," Mike said, shrugging his shoulders to indicate he did not have an answer.

Patrick paused to think. "We'll just have to deal with that when it happens," he said with resignation. "We have too many other things to worry about with adding that to the list."

"Yeah," Kwasi said with a smile, putting an end to this troubling thought. "Rahght now, you, Nick and Ah hab to make a longer ngoni and some more drums. Ah wanna hear you play music. Ah wann teach you some African songs."

CHAPTER EIGHTEEN
KWASITON

Early in the morning the time travelers, the two flyers, and Kwasi met again. "Deh baby's mudder, she gibe me one of her tings dat keep her hands warm," Kwasi said holding up an animal skin mitten. Africa was warm and people didn't wear mittens. So, Kwasi didn't know the word. "Dis is all deh dog needs to find deh sled."

Mike tied the rope around his waist. Allie, Patrick, and Jen did the same. "There's no need for all of us to go find the sled," Nick said. "I think Lenore and I, Lt. Newcomb and Ensign Dubois should stay here. You're going to bring in a lot of people. There aren't enough huts for them all. We need to build more."

"Deh women know how deh huts are made," Kwasi said. "Dey helped me. Dey know how to put up deh poles and how to cut deh grass for deh roof and sides. Ask dem to help you." He tied the rope to himself and the leash to Menlo. "Here, dog. Smell dis," he said, holding the mitten up to Menlo's nose. "Go fahnd it." Menlo led the line of people out the doorway into Nowhere.

An hour later the search team came back with the dog sled and a team of eleven huskies. The time travelers followed Kwasi as he took the dogs down to the stream for a drink. He left them in their harness to keep them under control. He threw them meat and bones from the animals he had hunted. The Inuit woman came to see the dogs. They recognized her and wagged their tails to say hello. Meanwhile, the time travelers and Menlo sat on the grass to watch.

When the dogs were watered and fed Kwasi put a leash around the lead dog's neck. "Ah teach him first," Kwasi told the time travelers. "He is deh lead dog. Deh udder dogs follow him. If Ah teach him, he will help teach dem. Dey will learn faster dat way." He let the dog out of   his harness.

The dog did not like the leash. He was a sled dog. He would wear a harness, but he refused to have anything around his neck. The dog struggled and growled and bit the leash. He tried to bite Kwasi. The rest of the dogs watched. They grew agitated and they began barking. Both Kwasi and the time travelers knew they were learning the wrong lesson. Kwasi had to win this contest, or none of the dogs would be any good for searching.

Menlo stood up. His ears were pinned back against his head and his J shaped tail was straight. Suddenly, he ran straight at the Husky and slammed his shoulder into the other dog. The lead dog fell over. Peeling back his lips to reveal his fangs, Menlo seized the Husky by the throat. The lead dog struggled, but Menlo bit all the more forcefully. Knowing he was completely at Menlo's mercy, the dog gave up and went limp. He knew Menlo could kill him by crushing or tearing his throat. He whined like a puppy to tell Menlo he had surrendered.

Menlo released the Husky and stepped back. He growled and then barked three times at the lead dog. Next, he turned and barked at the rest of the dogs. It was an angry bark and a warning. The lead dog stood, but hung its head. He was beaten and the fight was out of him. He was ready to do whatever Kwasi required.

Menlo trotted back to Mike and sat beside him. Mike put his arm around his Foxhound and hugged him. "You've been my dog since you were a puppy," Mike said. "You can do all kinds of things I never dreamed of. I'm going to call you Menlo the Wonder Dog." Menlo lapped Mike's face once and went back to watching Kwasi work with the Husky.

Two days later Kwasi and Patrick took the lead dog on a search mission while Mike and Allie went with Menlo. Ten other search teams went out, each led by a newly trained sled dog. Day after day, the teams left in the morning and returned later with groups of wanderers. The teams turned the newcomers over to Lt. Newcomb and Ensign Dubois. Then, they went back into Nowhere to find more people.

Lt. Newcomb and Ensign Dubois sat on the grass with those that were newly arrived and explained to them what had happened. The people had gotten lost in Nowhere, they had wandered for decades, even centuries. They had been rescued and would be living in a new world. Most of the people cried and grieved for their homes and families. The two flyers had gone through this. They comforted the people and gave them all the time they needed to adjust.

The next stop for the newcomers was Charmaine and her helpers. They asked each person to recall all the people who had been on their ship or plane. They made long lists of names. Charmaine checked off those that had been found. This way, she knew who was still missing.

Friends and family arrived from the village, so newcomers were greeted and welcomed by people they knew. Some reunions were very happy. The Inuit woman found her husband. He hugged her and the baby. Sally and Elizabeth's father, Captain Stevens, was found. Soon after, their sister Jane came in with a search party. Some reunions did not happen, leaving other people sad and afraid. The girls and their father greeted each search party, hoping this one had found their mother. Day after day, she remained lost.

After meeting with the two flyers and then with Charmaine, the newcomers went to the village where they welcomed as part of the growing population. Most went to work helping the women build new huts. Some of the people from Nowhere had been farmers. They went to work preparing land for Dr. MacDonald's seeds.

At night, the time travelers, Kwasi, Lt. Newcomb and Ensign Dubois, would meet to discuss the day, and plan for the next. "The row of huts was getting too long," Nick reported. "People living at one end of the road would never get to know the people living at the other. So, we started a new row next to the first one. Then, we realized we're building a village. By the time we're done, this will be a town. Lenore and I decided to draw up a plan for the new streets." Nick unfolded a big piece of paper with a map of the new town on it. He passed it to the others to examine. "We made all the streets begin in the middle at a town square, a big open space. We figure the towns folk can gather there. They can use it as a market or a meeting place. No one's hut will be far from the square."

"We named the town," Lenore said. "We decided it should honor the guy that founded it. We call it Kwasiton." Everyone nodded. That was a good name. Kwasi was embarrassed. "All of you helped make this town possible too" Lenore said to the others. "So, we named streets after each of you," "Newcomb Street, Dubois Street, Weaver Street, Canfield Street, etc."

A week later Patrick reported to the nightly meeting, "We're running out of people in Nowhere. Charmaine's list tells us only a couple of dozen people are still lost. We need to cut back on the number of search teams and use those people in more productive ways. Nick, you and Lenore should use half the dogs to get supplies from the ships and planes. It'll be a big job and you'll need a lot of people. I suggest you choose the strongest ones to work with you."

Now, teams started to bring back equipment. Nick had them store it outside the town where he could make an inventory. His teams brought electrical generators, electric motors, gasoline motors, tools, wire, and pipes - anything they could use. They brought food, medical supplies, and even books. They brought sheets, pillows, and extra cloths. They brought cooking equipment: pots, pans, plates and glasses. They brought tables and chairs. "We're stripping those boats bare," Nick told the others.

Teams brought in cows, pigs and chickens. One team brought back an entire airplane. It was the one Mike had examined, the civilian plane that had gotten lost on a trip to Bermuda. Several strong men lifted the tail and pushed it on its wheels, like a giant wheelbarrow. "We should get the Avengers," Lt. Newcomb said with excitement. "They're heavier, and it will take more men to roll them."

"Kwasiton will be the first town in the new world with its own Air Force," Ensign Dubois joked.

"I was thinking we could use the planes to explore this world," Lt. Newcomb answered. "Kwasi, you said you dream about flying like a bird. I'm gonna make that dream come true. I'm gonna take you flying with me. We'll find out what's on the other side of those hills."

A couple of nights later Mike reported to the group. "There are so few people left in Nowhere the search teams aren't saving anyone anymore. Unless a person pops up right next to a team, we can't get to them. They disappear before we can rescue them. They're always above us or below us."

"Use the ladder," Nick told Mike. "I brought a ladder so you can climb up or down to them. Have someone hold the ladder and climb it."

"Good idea," Allie said. "The guy who's really a problem is the runner." Those who had been on search teams nodded. It would be hard to save that guy. When he got lost he had been scared and took off running. He had been running in Nowhere ever since. He would pop up and run by the search teams. He was gone before they could move to save him.

The next day Mike and Allie tied themselves to Menlo and carried the ladder into Nowhere. It was strange to still hear the voices but not see anyone. They realized those voices would continue calling in Nowhere forever. At last, they saw Mrs. Stevens, the girls' mother wandering above them. She was upside down. She still had her hands to her mouth, silently calling her children. "You're smaller than I am, Allie," Mike said. "I'll hold the ladder for you." He pointed the ladder ahead of the woman so Allie would end up in front of her. The woman would walk into Allie's arms. He braced the ladder while Allie climbed it.

The ladder wasn't long enough. Allie stood at the top and watched the woman walk by overhead. Allie was curious. She put a foot off the ladder, but didn't fall. She put her other foot next to the first. She was still holding the ladder with her hands, but her feet were standing next to it. She let go. Now, she was standing above Mike. "Climb up," She told Mike as she held the top of the ladder to steady it.

Mike climbed up and stepped off next to Allie. "Weird," he said. "Just plain weird." The two pulled up the ladder and ran to get ahead of the woman. Mike put up the ladder again. Again, he pointed it in front of the woman and Allie climbed to the top. It would be close. Not enough. The top of the woman's head was passing just over Allie's hand. However, the woman's blond hair was tied up in a bun that stuck up (or in this case down) a little above her head. The small time traveler stretched her arm as far as she could and was able to pinch the bun with her fingertips.

As soon as Allie touched the woman she came out of Now and could see. She was scared. "Don't be afraid, Mrs. Stevens," Allie said. "You're safe. Your family's safe. We're going to take you to them." She gently pulled the woman down and handed her to Mike. "We should return her right away," Allie said to Mike. "Her family has been waiting a long time and they're worried."

"Take us back, Mennie," Mike said to his dog. He and Allie were amazed when Menlo walked straight ahead and out the doorway. "How come we didn't have to climb back down the ladder?" Mike asked.

Mike and Allie used the ladder trick to save more people. The runner ran by them several times, but they could never reach him. They saw two other people who were always too far away.

"Allie and I are not having any luck," Mike told the group at an evening meeting. "Charmaine's list tells us there are three people left in there. We've given up on the runner. The other two haven't popped up close enough to grab them."

"We're running out of time," Allie added. "That doorway is going to shut in a couple of days. I can't handle the thought of leaving those people in Nowhere, trapped forever. Does anyone have any ideas?"

The others all stared at the ground and shook their heads. Looking down, Nick noticed a hollow log and watched a spider weave a web over the end. He shook his head too. Nope. No ideas.

"We still haven't found our doubles," Allie noted. "I don't think they're in Nowhere, but I don't know what happened to them."

"For there to be two us in Nowhere we would have to be in two places at once," Mike replied. "There would be distance between us. There are no dimensions in Nowhere and it is not a place; I think we just merged with our doubles. That's my best guess."

"I'll take it," Patrick said. "That's one less headache."

The meeting ended. Mike and Patrick stayed behind talking to each other. A group of men approached them. Some of the men were wearing clothes like American colonists, socks and knee pants, with big buckles on their shoes. The others wore a gray uniform that Mike recognized. They were Confederate soldiers. "Sir," said one of the soldiers addressing Patrick. The soldier had sergeant stripes on his shoulder. Mike knew that being an officer; the group had asked him to speak for them. "Sir, you seem to be in charge here," the soldier said. "My friends and I are not happy, and we want to tell you why."

Patrick looked the man in the eye to show he was listening. "Sir, I am a Confederate soldier. We were smuggling guns to the Confederacy from Bermuda when we got lost. We would have used those guns to fight the Yankees. The Yankees are trying to end slavery. We are fighting to keep it. Sir, my men and I cannot take orders from a black man. It is not natural that a black man would tell a white man what to do. We won't have it!"

"Sir," one of the men in colonial clothes said to Patrick. "I am a slaver. We were bringing that man Caesar, Kwasi, whatever you call him now, and those women to Bermuda to their new master. My men and I, we order slaves what to do. They don't tell us."

Patrick slowly scanned all the men, looking each in the eye. "You disgust me," he said, spitting out the words. "Gentlemen, this is a new world, with new rules. Get used to them." Patrick turned and walked off leaving Mike with the soldiers and the slavers.

"Patrick can be blunt and short tempered," Mike explained to the group. "However, he is right."

"You don't understand, Sir," the soldier complained. "Your friend is asking too much of us. I don't hate black people, but they are not our equals. God made them to serve white people."

"I whipped that man, Kwasi," the slave driver said. "Do you know what he'll do to me if he's left in charge?"

"I know he has been whipped," Mike replied. "I've seen his scars. Listen. I'll try to explain things more clearly. As I see it, you men have three choices. You can go back into Nowhere. If you do, you'll wander for the rest of eternity." The men looked down. They didn't like that idea. "You can leave Kwasiton and live somewhere else. If you do, you'll probably starve to death." Some of the soldiers shook their heads. They didn't like that idea either. "Finally, you can do as Patrick said and get used to the new world and the new rules," Mike concluded. "To do that, you need to change your thinking. You can manage if you try.

"As for you," Mike said to the slaver. "I know Kwasi. He's kind, gentle, and forgiving. He won't hold that whipping against you. I advise you to apologize to him and tell him you want to help build a new world where everyone is equal. He will become your friend."

CHAPTER NINETEEN
THE WEDDING

The next morning Nick approached Mike and Allie just as they were getting ready to set off on another search mission. He carried a box under his arm. "Let me go with you," he said "I've got an idea." Nick opened the box. "Yesterday, I watched a spider weave a web, and it made me think," he said. "A web is a sticky trap. Bugs that touch the web get caught, and the spider comes back later to get them."

He opened the box. "Duct tape," he announced. "My Grandpa told me duct tape fixes everything. We're going to use the tape to weave a web in Nowhere. I'm hoping the last three people will wander into the tape web and get stuck. We can come back tomorrow and get them. We need to anchor the web. I'll start here by sticking one end on the CT 9225. Mike, take Menlo and find the Auckland. Stick the other end of the roll to it."

The next day Mike and Allie went through the door way into Nowhere. They found the last three people, even the runner, stuck to the web. One by one they freed them and brought them to Kwasiton. "We'll check the web one more time before the doorway closes," Mike told Patrick and Jen and the other time travelers. "Just in case there's still someone in there who isn't on Charmaine's list."

"Right," Patrick agreed. "We only have a couple more days to get out ourselves. We should be leaving soon."

Charmaine burst into tears. "I'm not going," she said.

Everyone was stunned and stared at her. "You can't stay," Patrick said awkwardly. "You have to come back with us." Lenore and Jen put their arms around Charmaine's shoulders to comfort her.

"No, I don't," Charmaine said to Patrick. "I don't have to go, and I'm not."

"Why do you want to stay?" Mike asked.

"I love Kwasi and I want to be with him. He loves me too. He asked me to marry him. That's what I want to do."

"Aren't you a bit young to get married?" Nick asked.

"Kwasi says girls marry young in his village. He says I'm old enough to be his wife."

"What about your family back home?" Patrick asked. It was awkward for the boys to ask these personal questions, but they were groping, trying to understand what had just happened.

"I'm an orphan," Charmaine answered. "I don't have any family. That's why the Smiths took me in. No one will miss me."

"What about the Time Institute. They can't just have a cadet disappear," Mike said.

"I'll ask Dr. Newcomb to tell everyone she transferred," Jen told Mike. Here was another surprise for the boys. The girls seemed to know all about this love between Kwasi and Charmaine, and had taken Charmaine's side.

Patrick looked at Mike. Mike shrugged. Patrick looked at Nick. Nick did the same. "Mr. Stevens is a ship's captain," Mike said. "Ships' captains can marry people."

"I don't know...." Patrick hesitated. He still didn't like this idea. He looked at the others, his gaze moving from one person to the next. No one agreed with him. "Oh, all right," he said giving in. Jen ran up to him and kissed him.

"You're a good guy, Patrick Weaver," she said proudly.

The next day the village gathered for a wedding. The men had set up long tables in the square for the wedding banquet. Women had brought lots of food and drink. Everyone was washed and wore the best clothes they had. Mr. Stevens was standing on a box with a Bible in his hands. It had paper markers at the verses the couple wanted him to read. Kwasi stood nervously next to the captain. Lt. Newcomb was Kwasi's best man. Patrick, Nick, and Ensign Dubois were the groomsmen.

Jen, Lenore, and Allie were the bridesmaids. Jane, Sally, and Elizabeth were the flower girls. One by one, the bridesmaids walked down the street to the square and stood on Captain Stevens' other side. They smiled across the makeshift aisle at the boys and the two Navy flyers.

Mike was standing nearby with Kwasi's donso ngoni. While he waited for the bride he reached under his uniform shirt and pulled out the locket Allie had given him just before he left on his first mission. Back then, the two did not know if they would ever see each other again. Mike opened the locket and gaze at the picture inside. It was a picture of him with Allie in the cadet dorm common room. Jen had pointed a camera at them. Before she snapped the photo Mike put his arm around Allie and pulled her toward him and the two touched their heads together. Allie had engraved Remember Me on the inside of the locket cover, opposite the picture.

Mike never removed the locket. He wore it even when showering and sleeping. When he was not with Allie, he opened it several times a day to stare at her face. A deep sadness swept over him as he looked at it now. For them, this day could never happen. He and Allie could never marry. The experience of time made it impossible for people from different times to be together. One would be cursed and remain forever young while the other aged and eventually died. The curse would continue as the one in the wrong sequence was eventually forced to bury the couple's children.

Some of the African women stepped out of a hut, a signal that the wedding was about to begin. Charmaine followed them, wearing her wedding gown. The women had sewn it for her with cloth cut from a white bed sheet. They had woven flowers in her hair and had given her a bouquet of flowers to carry. The whole town gasped at how beautiful she looked. Kwasi smiled widely and proudly and lots of people began to cry. They pulled out handkerchiefs and wiped their eyes and blew their noses. Many of the people crying were tough, hard working men; sailors, fishermen, and soldiers.

Mike returned his locket inside his shirt and started playing Here Comes the Bride as Charmaine began a slow march through the crowd, eventually arriving in front of Mr. Stevens. Kwasi took a step to his left so he stood beside her. "Dearly beloved," Mr. Stevens began.

After the wedding the townsfolk gathered for the feast. Patrick had made a sign with the name Sirens on it and attached it to a stake driven in the ground in front of their instruments. He, Nick, and Mike were the band. During the feast they played some of their own songs, songs they had written. When people had finished eating Mike decided it was time for some fun and some dancing.

"We're going to play an Irish wedding song," He told the crowd. "It's a real fast and happy song. You sailors know how to dance the jig. I want you to dance for us."

"We soldiers know how dance a jig too," The Confederate sergent yelled. "We'll challenge you sailors."

Mike smiled with satisfaction. He knew what this gesture meant. The sergeant and his soldiers had decided to join the new world and become good citizens. "Okay everyone," Mike yelled to the crowd. "You all be the judges. Cheer for who dances best, the sailors or the soldiers."

Patrick tapped out the beat. Mike and Nick picked up the fast lively tune while Mike sang,

"Step we gaily on we go,
heel and heel and toe for toe.
Arm and arm and row and row,
all for Charmaine's wedding.

"Over hillways up and down,
myrtle green and bracken brown,
Past the shiellings through the town
all for the sake of Charmaine.

"Step we gaily on we go,
heel and heel and toe for toe,
Arm and arm and row and row,
all for Charmaine's wedding.

"Plenty herring, plenty meal,
plenty peat to fill her kreel,
Plenty bonnie babes as well,
that's the toast for Charmaine."

The sailors and the soldiers danced with all the energy they had. Mike held his hand over the sailors. Half the crowd cheered. He held his hand over the soldiers. The other half cheered. "I call it a tie," Mike announced. Everyone cheered for the tired dancers who all fell on the grass to recover.

Next, Mike played a song Kwasi had taught him. It was about a brave hunter who married a beautiful woman. Mike's accent might not have been great, but the African women didn't mind. They knew this song. They formed a circle and danced to the music while the crowd clapped. Jen, Lenore, and Allie watched for a while until they had figured out the steps. Then, they joined in the dance. Other women from the town stepped into the circle and soon, all the women in Kwasiton were dancing. The Stevens sisters, Sally, Jane, and Elizabeth danced with them.

In the afternoon the townsfolk relaxed. They had danced all they could and they were tired. Groups of them sat on the grass talking and laughing. The Stevens girls played with Menlo and the Inuit baby. The time travelers sat by themselves and watched the people of this new town that had sprung up so quickly. "You know what this reminds me of?" Mike asked. "Hilton and New Durham. All three places were small towns. In all three places we had picnics and parties together. I like small towns like this. They're nice places to live." Allie put her head on his shoulder. Lenore took Nick's hand. Jen kissed Patrick.

A while later Patrick said, "I hate to be the party pooper, but this is a good time for us to sneak away. The doorway will close tomorrow."

Mike called Menlo. The time travelers quietly walked to the doorway and to the waiting CT 9225. The boys picked up their time craft to carry it to the other. "Mennie, find the Auckland," Allie told the dog.

▲

The boys stayed at the Time Institute for several days. The six time travelers met with Dr. Newcomb and Rabbi Cohen in Room 307 and told the teachers how they had helped establish Kwasiton. They said they had faith that Kwasi, Charmaine, and the two flyers would get things off to a good start. "Who knows," Rabbi Cohen said. "Maybe someday the people on that new world will find a way to visit the old world. It would be nice to learn how they made out."

▲

Mike, Nick, and Patrick returned to the Castleton house from their Saturday morning walk in the woods. "How did your GPS work?" Mrs. Castleton asked her son.

"Great," Mike replied. "We could find our way anywhere we wanted to go."

"Patrick, Nick, I promised your parents I would bring you home," Mrs. Castleton said. "Why don't you get in the van?"

"What are we doing tonight," Mike asked his mother as they walked to the car.

"Your father has selected a movie," Mrs. Castleton answered. "It's one of those 1940s black and white mystery movies."

"Those old movies are fun," Mike said enthusiastically. "Which one is it?"

His mother answered, "Return from Nowhere."

SAMPLE CHAPTER FROM BOOK FIVE OF THE CASTLETON SERIES

Chapter One
The Triumvirate

"Alayniess! Oh, Alayniess! Eternal city. You are so old no one knows when you came to be, or who built you. You have always been, and we thought you would last forever. Now, I am all alone to witness your end, and what I see has broken my heart." Carolus Nukium sat on the top step of a wide, stone staircase that led up to a large stone building.

Carolus was middle aged. His wavy hair was dark brown, with streaks of gray on his temples and around his ears. His bushy mustache had streaks of gray in it as well. He was a short man, around five feet tall. Seeing his face, you would know right away that he was usually a happy man. The pattern of lines at the corners of his eyes and mouth indicated that he spent most of his time wearing a broad smile. Not today. He held his face in his hands and was crying.

The building behind Carolus was in the center of a magnificent city. The staircase he sat on rose so high he could see his city stretched out below him. As high as he was, he could not see the city's end. It was that big. The most beautiful and famous cities in history – Athens and Rome – would not be built for another 10,000 years, but if their builders could have visited Alayniess, they would have burned with jealousy. The Greeks and Romans worked in white marble, a soft stone that is easy to cut and carve. Marble will last for many thousands of years. Alayniess was built of polished granite, one of the hardest of all stones. Granite will last forever. An eternal city has to be built of granite.

Granite is found all over the world. Large blocks of it are cut from mountain sides to be made into building materials. The site where granite is cut is called a quarry. Each quarry produces its own colors and patterns. People who work with this stone can look at a piece of granite and tell what country it came from, sometimes even the specific quarry. The people who built Alayniess used these different colors and textures to create buildings so beautiful they could only be believed by seeing them. To obtain different patterns Alaynians had searched the world. They brought back massive slabs of different colors and patterns of granite to their continent to create their city.

The building standing behind and above Carolus was obviously an important one. Anyone looking at it knew it was either the government center or a temple, as it was topped by a large, ornate dome, made of yellow granite. The stone was as smooth as glass and reflected the tropical sun. It was so brilliant the building looked like a star come down to earth.

Although Carolus was crying, he had not come to this place to weep. He had come to beg, to beg one last time for his city. Once again, he had been turned away and his emotions had overcome him. He sat on a granite step and his grief poured out of him. He raised his head from his hands and with red, swollen eyes, stared at the activity in the open plaza below him. There, a group of Alaynians were moving a massive granite block as big as two school busses. They went about their work as if nothing was wrong.

The Alaynians did not pull the huge stone blocks with ropes, like in the pictures of Egyptian workers building the pyramids. Instead, four Alaynians, one standing at each corner, guided the block with a stick-like tool. The granite block floated above the ground at about waist level, and glided slowly forward. When its path needed to be corrected, the four Alaynians moved their wand-like tools and the block responded.

The granite block was bright green. It was not shaped like a big brick, with straight sides and square corners. Instead, it resembled a piece to a gigantic, three-dimensional jig saw puzzle. When the four Alaynians reached the wall where it was to fitted, they raised their wands. This elevated the massive granite piece upward until it was slightly higher than an opening of the same shape. Then, the four workers used their wands to move the block precisely over the opening. Finally, they slowly lowered it into place. The block fit into the wall so perfectly the joints between the new piece and those already in place, disappeared. The texture and color of the granite block matched perfectly the color and texture of the wall. The building under construction looked like it was a single surface of unbroken granite.

Carolus turned his head to watch the work going on at a second construction site near the first. In this site, three statues were being carved in gray granite. The statues were as high as church steeples and stood in a row overlooking the plaza below. Even though they were incomplete, enough work had been done so Carolus knew who the statues honored. The two end statues were women, while the one in the middle was a man. All three looked so much alike there could be no doubt; the people they represented were closely related. Perhaps even sisters and a brother.

The carvers held rods like the ones being used by the workers moving the large building block, only these rods were shorter. The carvers used their rods to carefully slice away granite from the statues. For them, carving granite was like an ice sculptor using an electric chain saw to carve a block of ice. The rods sliced through the hard, dense stone as easily as a knife cuts through butter. The rods left behind a smooth, polished surface that needed no additional work.

"Alayniess, Alayniess," Carolus lamented. "Your art and your science almost equal those of the gods. Look what we have created. Look at what we can do. We have harnessed nature, and nature herself has become our servant. She does as we command. We tell stones to move and they obey. How could a civilization as beautiful and advanced as ours come to this bitter end?" He burst into tears again. He placed his face in his hands and tears trickled between his fingers.

"Eternal city, your republic is as old as you," he said as he wept, his body shaking with the violence of his sobs. "We governed ourselves and every Alaynian was free. We protected our liberty and would let no one take our freedoms from us. There is no one on this earth who could destroy us from without. Who would have ever dreamed that the end would come from within? Oh Alayniess, your own children have betrayed you!"

He lifted his red, tear-stained face and looked over his shoulder at the domed building behind him. He paused a long minute before standing and climbing the last two steps. This placed him on a wide granite platform in front of the yellow colored building.

Carolus walked to the building until he reached a line of Alaynian men standing shoulder-to-shoulder, the length of the platform. They were all the same size as Carolus, about five feet tall. He put his face right up to another man's, so he was staring his fellow directly in the eye. Normally, two people would find it uncomfortable to be this close to one another. However, the man did not respond. He stared straight ahead. He only reacted when Carolus tried to slip between him and the man next to him. Then, the two men linked arms and shifted their legs so they crossed, one man's leg overlapping the other's. At the same moment the entire line did the same thing, so like soldiers snapping to parade rest the long line became a human chain link fence. By joining their arms and crossing their legs, they closed any opening between them. As a result, Carolus could not pass anywhere along the platform. He was barred from the building by a living barrier of connected bodies.

Carolus moved down the line looking one man after another directly in the eye. None of them looked back. They all continued to stare straight ahead. Carolus came to a man he recognized. "Meekaylus," he said to his old friend. "Meekaylus, it is I, Carolus. Don't you recognize me? Our fathers were best friends. We grew up together. We have known each other all our lives. You married my sister. Speak to me, Meekaylus. You can break this trance. You are not a slave. You and I are free Alaynians." Meekaylus did not respond.

While Carolus was speaking to his mute brother-in-law, a flurry of activity and movement occurred behind the line of men. Three people had come out of the domed building and were separated from Carolus only by the row of bodies. The new arrivals were two women and a man. The three looked so much alike there was no doubt they were brother and sisters. They were all the same age, and so could be nothing other than triplets. The women were so beautiful that a man seeing them for the first time would gasp. As for the man, he was so handsome all women would welcome his attention. Carolus did not react to their appearance. He knew the three, and was not affected by their beauty.

"Carolus Nukium," said one of the women, her voice dripping with sarcasm. "You are so tiresome. I don't have to ask why you have come back. It's for the same reason you have visited us before: time, after time, after time. You want the Triumvirate to stop its progress and give back your precious republic. It is not going to happen. Alayniess belongs to us now, as do the Alaynians. We are building an empire that will be far more glorious than the old republic. We are not going to stop because of your endless begging. So, stop. You sound like an annoying sea bird– pleeez, pleeez."

Carolus threw himself against the line of men. Their linked arms and crossed legs acted like a trampoline. He merely bounced off them. The men did not even blink. They just stared ahead. "Ha," the man with the two women laughed at Carolus' futile efforts. "Carolus, take my advice. The time has come for you to leave Alayniess. You don't belong here anymore. We don't know why you are not in a trance. Why out of all the people in Alayniess, are you alone immune? However, even if you are unaffected, you can't stop us. Since you find our empire so distasteful, why don't you go to the snowy lands to the east?

Join those other types of men that live in caves and wear animal skins? They attach sharp stones to the ends of sticks to hunt meat. Maybe they will take you in and teach you how to sharpen a stone. Then, you can come back with weapons and try to stop the Triumvirate. Or, you could stay with them and build a republic for them. I'm sure a republic would appeal to people so primitive. They don't have the intelligence to understand the glories of an empire. You'll fit right in."

"Congrata, Exeta, Lexitus," Carolus said, holding his hands together as if praying. "I knew you as children. Please listen to me. Alayniess educated you, nurtured you, and raised you. You have always held such promise. Even when you were young, it was obvious you had been blessed with great ability. You could have been honored and respected servants of your city and your people. I don't know what causes this trance. I only know you are using it to control Alaynians. I don't know why I don't go into the trance so that you can't control me. I don't know why you three don't go into the trance. I don't why those who live in the country don't go into the trance, unless they come into Alayniess. But, I beg you. Stop what you are planning. Work with me to free our fellow Alaynians from the trance and to return their freedom to them."

"We are doing something even greater," the woman Exeta replied. "Although you do not think so, the Triumvirate does serve Alayniess. We are making Alayniess even greater than she was under the republic."

"Your Triumvirate serves the Triumvirate. You are glorifying yourselves," Carolus argued. "Alayniess never built statues to honor those who serve the city. Now, you are erecting statues to yourselves, statues taller than most buildings. This is ego. This is pride. This is not the service Alaynians have always given freely and without payment. This is control, not the freedom Alaynians have always enjoyed."

"I will tell you one final time, Carolus," the man Lexitus said, anger replacing his earlier mocking tone. "Leave

Alayniess! You don't belong here anymore. Go make your life elsewhere, perhaps with the primitives. If you stay here you will go on being miserable for the rest of your life. However, you will never be able to stop the Triumvirate. We are too powerful. Go!"

The two women and the man turned and reentered the building. Carolus returned to his step, sat down, and began to cry again. Again, he sobbed so forcefully that his whole body shook.

ABOUT THE AUTHOR

Mike Dunbar began writing as a 19-year old cub reporter. Since then, he has published seven books and written more magazine articles than he can remember. His name has been on the mastheads of three national magazines. He has been a newspaper and magazine columnist, and an editor. He has hosted a radio and a television show. He is in demand as a seminar speaker. He lives in Hampton, NH with his family. He operates and teaches at The Windsor Institute, a school that specializes in handmade Windsor chairs, He blogs atmikedunbar.tumblr.com, windsorchairs.tumblr.com, andthewindsorinstitute.com/blog. He tweets at @Castleton series.

MORE BOOK BY MIKE DUNBAR

The End of Time, book three in The Castleton Series
The Lost Crew, book two in The Caslteton Series
The Hampton Summit, book one of The Castleton Series
The American Country Woodworker
Woodturning for Cabinetmakers
Restoring, Tuning, and Using Classic Woodworking Tools
Federal Furniture
Make a Windsor Chair
Windsor Chairmaking
Antique Woodworking Tools

OTHER BOOKS BY SOUL STAR
Angel's Dance
Book 2 in the Clear Angel Chronicles
By Heidi Angell

Psychic Clear Angel hasn't seen or heard from her one-time lover Detective Grant since their first case wrapped up six months ago, and that is perfectly fine with her! But when he shows up on her porch in the rain and in tears, she cannot hold her ground. No matter how she feels about Grant and

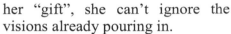

her "gift", she can't ignore the visions already pouring in.

Grant knows that he is no good for Clear, and has respected the distance she has kept. But when his daughter goes missing and the Chicago police have no leads, he turns to Clear and her unique abilities.

This next adventure puts Grant and Clear in close quarters as they find themselves once again fighting their feelings for one another. Thrust into the dark underworld of performance art, they strive to track down a ballerina who keeps taunting Clear in her visions. As they delve deeper into one studio, the grisly visions that haunt Clear may be more than she can handle. Can Clear hold it together to help find Grant's daughter before it is too late?

Available in e-book through Smashwords https://www.smashwords.com/books/view/374538 or your e-book retailer. Available in paperback through Amazon http://amzn.to/IJyUs3 or your local bookstore.

End of Time, Book Three in the Castleton Series
by Mike Dunbar

In the distant future, technology has disappeared and few humans remain. This remnant lives a simple, peaceful existence; until an unexpected invader arrives. Yellow in color, shaped like a cross between a knight in armor and a football player--- these beings liquefy all the people they find. The villagers call them Dandelions, because they are yellow in color and just popped up out of nowhere. Charlie Newcomb escapes these monsters and travels back seven generations to find the daring innovative time crew described in her ancestor's diary.

Freshly returned from studying the Battle of Agincourt for a UNH professor Mike Castleton, Patrick Weaver and Nick Pope witnessed the power of the English long bow. With this simple weapon, a handful of English archers had destroyed an army of French knights. The CT9225's crew answers Charlie's desperate plea for help. With their friends Allie Tymoshenko, Jen Canfield and Loren Smith they return with Charlie to lead the few unarmed humans into battle with the Dandelion army, and perhaps witness the end of time.

Available in e-book on Smashwords
https://www.smashwords.com/books/view/365147 or through your e-book retailer and in paperback
http://www.amazon.com/End-Time-Book-Castleton/dp/1492721751/ref=sr_1_1?s=books&ie=UTF8&qid=1386361260&sr=1-1&keywords=End+of+Time+by+Mike+Dunbar through Amazon or your local bookstore.

The Price of Honor
by Gus Gallows

Ganth, the Minotaur Empire, stretching across the continent of Ice Wall within the realm of Algoron, is a place where Honor is the foremost trait among its citizens. Here strength defines law; a law that has left Pah'min in disgrace. His life in Ganth forfeit, his childhood love denied; he is snubbed by all. But there is one House that will accept him. The secret house is despised as an honor-lacking abode of spies. It is from this dark place that Pah'min must begin the long and painful trek to restore his honor. He must begin again in the land of his enemies, and feign loyalty to a king he loathes. There will be many foes on all sides, but his greatest battles are within as the gods themselves try to sway him toward their own mysterious end. Ultimately, he must escape, sacrificing those he holds dear, all to pay the price.. The Price of Honor.

Available in e-book format through Smashwords https://www.smashwords.com/books/view/345472 or your local e-book retailer. Available in paperback through createspace https://www.createspace.com/4394101 or order through your local book store.

The Lost Crew
by Mike Dunbar

In book two of the Castleton series Allie, Jen, and their comrade Bashir are sent on a mission to study the roots of Jazz. They follow this music back through time -- from New Orleans, to Paris, and to ancient Carthage. Unbeknownst to the Time Institute the crew are captured and sold into the Roman Empire as slaves. Mike, Nick, and Patrick are recruited for their first rescue mission. They must retrace the lost crew's steps, discover what happened, and bring their fellow time travelers home. By the time they arrive will their friends be alive or dead? Can they be saved without changing time and setting off Chaos? Do their friends want to be saved? You'll discover once again that time travel messes with your mind and with your heart.

Available in paperback through Createspace
http://bit.ly/1e6FwKi or your local book dealer.
Available in e-book through Smashwords
http://bit.ly/18Ntk45 or your e-book retailer.

Elements of a Broken Mind
Book 1 in The Clear Angel Chronicles
By Heidi Angell

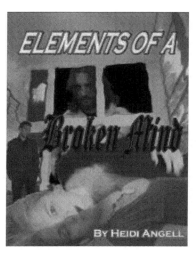

Grant Anderson is a small-town detective whose job was quiet and easy, until three girls end up dead. A serial killer is stalking the young ladies in his town. Without the high tech equipment of big cities at his fingers, Grant must rely on good old-fashioned police work; but with no discernible pattern and no clues to follow, the case seems to be grinding to a halt.

Then Grant gets a visit from a mysterious young woman. Who is Clear Angel? What is her connection to the case? If Grant is to believer her, then he must accept that she has "seen" these things. But Grant is a professional. He cannot believe in psychics! Yet when another girl goes missing, and Grant's search is yielding nothing he is desperate enough to try.

Grant and Clear team up to stop a madman bent on the destruction of the world. As their feelings for one another grow, they try to deny them. But when Clear goes missing, Grant must face his feelings and save her before it is too late.

Available in Paperback through Createspace
https://www.createspace.com/4302361 or your local book store.
Available in e-book through Smashwords
https://www.smashwords.com/books/view/325771 or your e-book retailer.

The Hampton Summit
Book 1 in The Castleton Series
by Mike Dunbar

Time travel messes with your mind, and your love life. That's what you'll discover in the Castleton Series, an eight-book romantic/adventure saga for smart, curious readers.

In The Hampton Summit, Allie and Mike meet when Mike and his friends are recruited by time travelers to prevent a murder in their hometown. A team of renegades from the Time Institute intends to kill a wheelchair-bound scientist before he can share a discovery that creates the peaceful future Allie knows. The assassins' goal is to rearrange the past so they can dominate the chaotic world they create. Traveling forward in time to be trained at the Institute, the boys are befriended by fellow cadets, Allie, and her roommate, Jen. Using only their wits, the group of innovative and resourceful teens risks their own lives as they take on the team of killers. In the process, Mike and Allie kindle a romance that can never be.

Available in Paperback from your local book store or Createspace https://www.createspace.com/4201346
In E-book formats through Smashwords
https://www.smashwords.com/books/view/296925 or your preferred e-retailer.

The Hunters
by Heidi Angell

What would you do if you found your town had been infested with vampires? For Chris and his brother Lucas, the answer was simple enough: you fight back. Gathering a small band of other people in their town who have been affected by the vampires, they begin a resistance. But after a year of fighting, they have only managed to kill a handful, while the vampire leader has turned five times that many.

Then two enigmatic strangers appear, changing the groups lives even further.

Fury and Havoc. They call themselves hunters, and want no part in this little band of heroes. Ordering them to lay low, the duo vow to rid their town of vampires. When Fury is injured, Chris aides these strangers, entwining his future with theirs.

Now that the vampires know the hunters are here, and that Chris and his friends have helped them, the group is in more danger than ever before. Lucas is torn between protecting his new family from the vampires, and protecting them from these seemingly inhuman beings who say they are there to help.

After all, what beings could be so powerful as to scare a vampire?

Available in paperback through your local book dealer or Createspace https://www.createspace.com/4112865
Available in e-book through Smashwords
https://www.smashwords.com/books/view/270492 or your preferred e-book retailer.

Angels & Warriors: The Awakening
by Dawn Tevy

In the novel, 'Angels & Warriors, The Awakening,' author Dawn Tevy introduces you to characters that are funny, loving, and artfully scheming... Our heroin, Lady Tynae, finds herself in a precarious situation when she is hunted down by those she most trusts. In a single heartbeat her fairly simple life becomes incredibly complicated. Finding herself in a new world full of magic, dragons, and an old friend, Tynae soon discovers nothing in her life was ever as it appeared. The vivid scenes and descriptive dialogue will transport you to another place. This spectacular fantasy world is set in a time and land that has slowly faded into the haziness of legend and lore. Between discovering her new world and falling in love, Tynae must uncover what lies at her very core. She is accomplished with swords, an expert marksman, and she even knows how to bring a full grown man to his knees...but is she the 'Chosen One'?

Available in paperback and E-book from Amazon
http://www.amazon.com/books/dp/0615602002

Made in the USA
Lexington, KY
27 March 2014